'Ffion' is a re-release of
'Tail of a Witch' book

Please look out for more books

Book 1: Ffion - Tail of a Witch

Book 2: Ffion - The Devils Game

Book 3: Ffion - Spirit of the Five Stones

Book 4: Ffion - The Dark Lights

Knoxxx

for more information go to -

www.tailofawitch.com
Instagram: tailofawitch
www.facebook.com/TailofaWitch

I

II

Information

All illustrations by: Paul Simpson

KDP ISBN: 9798500646200

IV

Forward
How Book 2 came to be

It wasn't long after making the decision to finally do something with the first story that one question was raised – What happens next to Ffion?

If you haven't read the first book yet then please don't read on if you don't want a spoiler.

With the events that took place at the end of book one there were gaps in the story that hadn't been covered by the last page. Although this was deliberate in order to get people asking 'what did her mother want at the end?' and 'what happens next to Ffion,' in order to spark peoples interests and imagination, I had no answer to give anyone.

It was while book one was being proofed that I gave any consideration of when people finished the book and asked 'so what happened next,' I have a reply other than 'I don't know.'

I started making notes on the where and why Ffion would need to leave and what her mothers request would be. Once I had this, then I needed reasons as to why things were happening what the end goal was. Having decided upon the plot I thought it would be good to have Ffion as the cameo in this story so it could be told in a different setting and atmosphere while giving it a solid link back to the first story. Due to the link that is made and the fact they are both set at Halloween was also the reason why both story's needed to come out as close together as possible. The tale in part for this setting is darker in tone than the previous and if Tail of a Witch was a PG movie then this would definitely be a 12A. I hope you enjoy the second adventure.

And thank you for coming back for round two.
P.Simpson

VI

Thanks and Acknowledgements

I would like to say thank you to those who have helped in getting this second book up and running and thank you to those reading.

I hope you enjoy the update of the new cover and story illustrations.

To all my family with love x

VIII

Contents

Ffion - the story so far.

Book 1: Tail of a Witch

On Halloween night a witch named Ffion is offered a deal by a shadowy figure with yellow glowing eyes to cast one of Hell's residents called Jack back into its darkest pit, but she must return him within 24 hours and the clock is ticking. Her only problem is that she was cursed over 300 years ago to wander the world as a cat. The reward for completion is release from this spell, however failure would result in the doorway to Hell staying open for all of its occupants to escape and wander the earth forever.

After a long fight in the attic of an old mansion, along with help from her cat friend George, Ffion was successful and defeated Jack and the power of the magic ember he carried, shattering it in to pieces and sending him back through the blue spinning portal he used to escape. As the clock struck midnight, the power of the portal closing destroyed the old Mansion which was swallowed into the ground. Escaping the building, Ffion's spell was broken just as the stranger had promised. Returning to visit her mothers spirit that is trapped within the standing stones on a nearby hill, she is given a new task that again, will affect her very future.

Ffion: Book2
The Devils Game

by Paul Simpson

Prologue
1am, November 1st

"Officer Hobs is that you?" shouted the reporter as he searched his pockets for anything to take a note with on the scraps of paper in his hand.

Hobs turned and rolled his eyes "Its two in the morning, I'm freezing out here all by myself and apart from what you can see without a flashlight and the fact I'm standing where a really large house use to be standing, how can I possibly help you Mckenzie?" he answered in a slightly sarcastic tone as he began to walk over to where Mckenzie stood.

Hobs waited as the reporter finally produced a pen from his jacket pocket, "Very funny Hobs, ha ha bet you're the life of the party. I only asked as I didn't see your car around but I heard your call out on the radio" joked Mckenzie back at him as he spoke out aloud as he began to write. "So, it's November 1st, A.M., there are people still out at parties or at least staggering back home from them, which is where I should be SO, what can you tell me about what happened here," he finally asked, his pen hovering anxiously over the notepad.

Hobs sighed "For your record, we have ourselves a little mystery to solve and it would be better if you didn't write anything until we know what were dealing with, plus the fact of what its got to do with you? Don't you report for the paper in the next town."

The reporter was amused by the latter fact "The same as it's got to do with you, officer who also comes from the same town. Don't you find it strange that there's no one here, in the entire village?"

The officer turned to look back over his shoulder, the village was empty with doors open, windows broken and some, but very few, lights still left on, as if everyone had either run away at the same time or simply disappeared in a single night.

Turning the other way Hobs looked over the remains of what should have been a mansion. Apart from the light of the full moon creeping from behind a cloud, the whole floor area was aglow with orange embers scattered about the ground like glitter.

Hobs turned his gaze back to the reporter "I don't know what happened here, but apart from being sent to find out what occurred you're the first person I've seen."

Mckenzie stepped forward to look at the glowing embers more closely. "What are these?" he asked Hobs.

"I don't know," he replied in a slightly hesitant manner "but I wouldn't touch it if I were you" he warned. Mckenzie seemed oblivious to the last comment as he crept ever closer to one of the fragments and reached out to pick one up.

The ember felt warm in his hand and gave off a bright orange radiance. The reporter inspected the piece closer, holding it between his fingers "You know it looks like burning wood but it feels smooth like a pebble, as if it was petrified, weird just, weird."

As he looked at it further he noticed the glow had spread into the tips of his fingers, he seemed transfixed as his skin burned but without pain, going from red to black and charred, but still he looked on. The burning had now taken his hand over as his skin cracked. The glow seemed to spread through charred channels the way molten lava would creep across the ground. The burning travelled onward under Mckenzies clothes appearing again from his shirt collar and moving through his body, slowly roasting him alive but still without the pain of heat, he was transfixed and unable to break his grasp. He looked over at the officer as if in disbelief as the final wave started to work its way up his neck and over his head. In the last few moments he turned his gaze back to the ember, not realizing it has fallen to the floor as his hand turned to ash. The look of panic fills his eyes as he looks upon officer Hobs who just

2

stood watching as a gentle breeze blows and Mckenzie, silently screaming, slowly drifts away like paper ash would in the wind.

Hobs walked over to the spot where Mckenzie had been standing. Two burn marks were scorched into the grass where his shoes had been minutes earlier. Bending slightly Hobs reached out to pick up the same ember, and, with a brief pause, grabs it. Hobs looks back at the spot on the floor, flicking the ember into the air with his thumb like a penny, "I told you not to touch it, but people just don't listen."

Picking up more of the larger pieces he presses them hard into his hand to create one larger quartz shaped shard. Examining it closely he holds the ember shard up, the glow now lighting his face. Staring intensely, his gaze is interrupted by movement on the next hillside. He looks over peering through the moonlit night at a formation of standing stones only to see the figure of a young woman staring back at him. She takes a few steps back after noticing that's she's being watched, she turns with a flash of light, a cat is now in her place which runs off into the cover of night.

Again Hobs smiles a wry grin. Suddenly from behind him comes a noise, this time the drum of helicopter blades beating the air. The clouds swirl in the downdraft as two more helicopters turn their spotlights on the officer, who quickly drops the large shard.

Several security detail, all dressed in body armour with weapons surround him screaming at him, "Drop to your knees and hands in the air, NOW, NOW," Hobs stares back, unnerved by what is taking place as he slowly lowers to his knees and places his hands behind his head. Watching patiently he observes a third helicopter land as what seems to be a research team disembark. With white suits and full head gear they begin setting about with long claws on handles to collect the orange ember shards one at a time. The main research scientist makes his way over to the circle of security. Reaching down with his gloved hand, he

3

picks up the large ember by the side of the officer. Like a radio speaker the voice from the man inside the masked suit speaks.

"I'll get this bagged up with the rest of the science team, the rest of you secure the area and…" he pauses as if making a decision.

"Bag him and bring him with us."

Hobs looks around as, from behind him, one of the security team takes the butt of his gun and knocks him out.

The sun breaks over the horizon in a golden blaze of light. Loading the unconscious officer aboard, the helicopters lift from the ground and scatter back into the safety of the night. The grounds of the old mansion house are left clear of any dangerous remains. The light of the new day reveals the devastation in the village. The sunlight showed the one thing left behind from the scene that the darkness had hidden. The light glares off bare metal, a lone police car lies on it side, crumpled from its fall down the hillside behind the mansion's grounds. From amongst the shadows, smashed glass and torn metal, lies the bloodied hand of the officer formally know as Hobs.

Chapter 1
The Journey Begins

Four years later, October 30th, 10.38pm.

The music from the night club blasted out at a deafening volume as the crowd danced the night away to the rock music. Over at the bar a group of friends were just starting to enjoy the night's entertainment. One young woman in her early twenties with auburn hair standing about 5'6" stands up from the group's chairs and quickly drinks up the orange juice left in her glass.

Her friends look up as one shouts out to her "HEY JODIE, let me get the next round in but something with a bit more kick to it eh?"

Jodie smiles and shouts back over the noise "I can't, I've got to go to work tonight."

"WHAT" shouts one of her group, "You've only been working there a few months and they got you pulling a late shift. Call in sick and stay with us, you're not exactly dressed for work are you?"

Jodie checks out her outfit "What's wrong with black boots and combat trousers," she questioned giving a twirl as she puts on an orange long sleeve jacket over a sleeveless black patterned zipped tank top, "It looks formal...... enough. Anyway once I have my work jacket on, no one will see! Besides, I need this job as I like to lie in mornings and stay up late, so it works perfectly. So, thanks for the drink in advance but I'm driving tonight. I'll be sure to take you up on the offer for tomorrows Halloween get together."

Hugging her closest pals Jodie leaves the club and goes out into the car park. Running over, she jumps in her car and with a turn of the ignition and a click of her belt she sets off out of town.

"Going to be late for work again eh Jo" speaking to herself in the car mirror as she speeds along the quiet country road reaching out to turn on the stereo which starts blasting out rock music. Deeper into the night she drove; the streetlights now far behind in the distance with just a full moon to light the way ahead. Taking a turn off into a forest she drives a few more miles before being stopped by a high built wall and security gates. A security camera fixed to the wall turns and looks at the car, Jodie rolls down the window and gestures to the camera to hurry up. With a clunk and a whirr the gate bolt opens and off she sped with a spin off tyres and grit toward the faint lights ahead of a large facility hidden deep within the forest.

With a screech of brakes from outside the window, the guards all turned to each other and gave a knowing nod and smile.
"One day that new girl might get her act together and actually turn up for work with time to spare," spoke one of the team, as they listened to the rapid footsteps race across the car park.
"I doubt it" laughed one of the others as they all turned to watch the entrance. The doors to the science facility's lobby burst open as Jodie ran past the security desk.
"Running late again Jodie" laughed the main guard on duty as the young woman skidded across the floor fumbling in her pockets for her swipe card.
"Hi Pete" she wheezed, trying to catch her breath "you know me, always like to keep things exciting" she panted as her hand shook holding her pass trying to swipe through the security door. Pete shouted from his desk "You'd better hurry, the experiment starts in four minutes. Nice outfit by the way, very suitable for work" he laughed.
Jodie grinned back "I knew there was a reason I loved the night shift, your constant positive attitude Pete" she laughed and pushed open the heavy metal security door. Racing through the large stark gray and white

9

Pete

my friend

Main door
guard at lab

corridors past office doors and dodging around members of staff, Jodie listened as the main announcement came over the various speakers and TV monitors dotted around the facility, 'Two minutes until the phase three experiment, all staff are required to attend their posts, two minutes'.

She raced over to a set of brightly coloured lockers which stood out like a sore thumb as much as her jacket did against the white wall and bright lighting, Jodie opened the door and threw in her bag and keys before grabbing her Lab coat and racing off again down more corridors to the main science block.

'One minute' came the announcement as she reached the second security door. This one was far more impressive than the lobby, much bigger and thicker resembling a bank vault and after swiping her pass again this much heavier door opened very slowly.

Over the speakers came another announcement '30 seconds until the midnight launch.'

Racing hard down the corridors, Jodie ran for the meeting room where the main experiment was being shown on a large monitor. Creeping in through the door into the darkened room she took a seat at the back as the head scientist came on the screen to begin the night's main task.

Chapter 2
The Experiment

The head of the science division Dr Mark Williams came on screen as his team made the final preparations behind him. Jodie had met him on very few occasions since she had started there, even then it was just in passing. He was about 5'10 with thinning short dark hair, clean-shaven with a stony faced demeanour. All he seemed to care about was his work and the project, she even wondered if he ever left the lower levels at all as his skin was so pale. With a cough he announced his intention to begin speaking.

"Good morning, I'd firstly like to thank you for your time and attention. To mark the recording, please note it is October 31st and the time is 12.03am. To those who are not familiar with this work I will cover the basics while the main team make the final checks. Four years ago we came into possession of this shard. The location of its procurement is currently classified. Over the last few years we have tried to run tests but it was soon found that the strange energy it gives off peaks by 3000% for only 24hrs a year on this exact date, as you can see behind me it has already started to give off a strong orange glow, it will stay this way until the exact second to midnight which is why we have started the experiment now. In order to maximise our time, to get tests completed and results compiled. I ask all of you within this facility to work hard and quickly or else we will have to wait another year for this opportunity."

Dr Williams moved away from the camera and toward the back of the table with the shard upon it. The team moved about taking readings and measurements bathed in the orange glow.

"As my team take the readings the information will be fed to the relevant offices where each sub-team is based. Once you have this please begin your designated projects" asked the doctor as he proceeded to work on the equipment around him.

Jodie's team received the first results and began scurrying about. Most of what was going on was above Jodie's understanding, her job as assistant was mostly leg work or doing as she was told when asked, so she knew for the short term there would be nothing for her to do but wait until she was needed. For now she continued to watch the large screen with great interest, wondering how such a small object could create this level of enthusiasm.

Once all the external readings had been taken it was now time to hook up it up to the machine and test if it could be used as a source of power. The doctor waved staff around the room to fetch different apparatus, Jodie watched as they all moved round like a rehearsed ballet of movement with perfect timing so not to waste a minute of precious time.

The doctor then asked for the first of the main tests to begin.

"First I will be conducting a test on various materials to see just what kind of power this shard produces."

This involved a simple battery charge reader. Upon placing the wires on to the shard the needle went straight to full power and then proceeded to heat up and smoke as the energy levels began to melt the device. Next was a simple light bulb, each time it was placed within the orange glow it would light up without any contact. The third test was a plant with an unopened flower bud, an odd choice thought Jodie but she continued to watch as they placed the plant near to the shard again. Slowly the bud lifted and began to open into full bloom. After a few more items the doctor announced the next phase.

"From initial readings it would seem the power this gives off can place energy into any mechanical or biological creation, natural and man made, quite amazing really. For the next part we will need to hook the

14

shard up for readings from our main computers."

The team set up the next round of experiments and wired up the shard to analyse. As the computer programmes started to run the shard suddenly lost its glow. Everyone stopped in the room and approached the desk, the doctor started to check the wires with some confusion wondering if it was something they had done or if it had been drained of power. Then with a surge of power the whole room was bathed in the bright orange glow, stronger than anyone had ever seen, causing the lab staff to cover their eyes as they took a few steps away from it. The wires linked to it crackled with energy as sparks flew through and up them toward the main computers. As the power hit the machines the room's lights blew out and the computers fizzed and crackled like a box of fireworks going off, while shouts and screams from the people came over the speakers. Jodie looked on in amazement and slightly worried, in fact it seemed the whole facility around her had stopped to watch the monitors of the live feed. The doctor came back on the screen within the orange glow of the shard as the dull backup lighting came on.

"Everyone I can see is fine" confirmed the doctor as he turned his attention back at the experiment and wondered, "It would seem the shard had a power surge of some description, given its tested capabilities I would not even rule out a basic intelligence, as if it knew and waited to be linked to the main systems otherwise why not cause the surge earlier?"

The doctor and his team set about again clearing the lab in order to continue with the reading when in the distance seemed to come a dull thud through the room. Again everyone stopped, the whole facility staff seemed to feel the vibration. The doctor waved over the security guards in the room, "Radio down to the tech lab and ask them if that tremor came from their section" he ordered. The head guard radioed down but with no reply, again he sent a call out, again nothing but a hiss of static. The doctor became more agitated at the lack of response.

15

"Send a team down to check it out."

The guard acted on the doctor's instructions and headed for the door calling over his radio "Security patrols we have lost contact with the tech division, guards 24, 26 and 32 meet me at the elevators for immediate inspection of the lower levels, guards 12 and 23 stay with the lab team and await instructions."

Everyone once again stared at the monitors as the guards ran out of the lab and the doctor set up a radio for communication updates just as a second ground shaking thud came through the building. Jodie had begun to feel a little uncomfortable as the events unfurled live on screen, what was worse was that it wasn't that far away from where she was sitting, just one floor down in a higher security part of the building.

Over the monitor feed the radio crackled again as everyone could hear what was being said.

"Doctor, we have reached the lower levels and it's a complete mess down here. Most of the lighting is out and I'm afraid most of the skeleton crew that were staffing tonight seem to be dead sir, several of them seem to have been crushed. Apart from that there's nothing down here to explain the mess and wha….! WAIT, movement down the corridor, moving to investigate. What is that! Looks like a huge ball. It coming this way, team open fire."

The radio in the doctor's hand exploded with the noise of gunfire from the security teams weapons. The head guard came over the speaker shouting over the noise of the guns "DOCTOR, IF YOU CAN HEAR ME, LOCK THIS FLOOR DOWN, WE ARE UNDER ATTACK, REPEAT WE ARE UNDER ATTAAAAAAAHHhhhhhhhh!"

The radio fell silent as staff began to panic at what they had just heard, so was Jodie as another louder, closer thud shook the floor. The doctor radioed through to the security quarters

"All teams we need a lock down on the tech level, hostiles reported before contact was lost."

16

Another loud thud shook the floor much closer now as even the wall monitors shook. Teams of guards were now in full gear running through the corridors to the elevators while the doctor signalled to his staff to pack up. From over at the table, still clearly on screen the shard began to pulse as another thud rocked the building. One of the lab staff brought the doctor's attention to the shard and he stopped and stared at it, drawn in almost hypnotised by it. A loud rumble came from behind the security doors as the two lab guards prepared their weapons. With a loud clang of metal on metal the lab door was hurled from one side of the room to the other taking the guards with it as their body muscles tightened causing them to squeeze the triggers of their machine guns sending a hail of bullets across the room with them striking several of the staff before landing on the far side of the lab knocking the camera over onto its side. More shots could be heard over the monitors live lab feed as peoples feet scrambled past the camera lens in a panic.

The doctor crawled on his hands and knees over to the camera in the glow of the shard, his face and coat splattered with blood, "If anyone is there please help us, PLEASE" he begged as a large metal fist came slamming down from behind over his head, crushing his skull with one blow, his now lifeless eyes staring into the camera as the large metal fist came down again in front of him cutting the link off with one final blow.

Chapter 3
The Escape

Jodie stood still staring at the video feed from the laboratory, the static fills the screen but the event seems to play over in her mind as if she can't possibly believe what she's just seen.

"Are they really all dead" she asks openly to anyone standing in the room but there is no one left to speak too. Snapping back in to reality she's stunned by the noise of the alarms as the orange warning lights rotate in the corner of the room. Out in the corridor are more lights, staff are seen running and screaming in every direction, Jodie peers around the doorway to watch the pandemonium taking place before her. Down to the left side of the corridor she can hear the echo of people shouting near the access lifts, "MOVE BACK TO THE RECEPTION WHILE WE TRY TO CONTAIN THE INCIDENT" shouted a voice of what she could only presume was the security team trying to blockade the lifts. Once again she could hear, "PLEASE MOVE AWAY FROM THIS SECTION AND GIVE US SPACE TO WORK. THIS AREA IS OFF LIMITS UNTIL THE SITUATION BELOW HAS BEEN DEALT WITH."

Jodie's curiosity grew as she edged her way towards the lift area to see what was happening. It was filled with staff, darting through office doors, some grabbing handfuls of research papers, others shouting at security that they had family and loved ones trapped on lower levels. With a loud echo from the lift shaft there came an almighty clunk as if a large metal weight had been dropped. The guards turned slowly to stare at the lift's buttons as the 'up' arrow light activated, the room fell silent and everyone watched the display as the numbers counted from the sublevels to ground floor. Jodie stared at the lift doors along with everyone else; the guards had now fully turned to aim their weapons at the doors as they edged the crowd back into the hallways, all waiting in the encompassing silence.

BANG! went the lift doors as they flew from their fixings squashing several people against the wall so hard that the sound of bones cracking could be heard over the following screams. People began to run as the security team opened fire into the lift. A huge metal hand extended out of the lift and crashed heavily down to the floor as the bullets ricocheted off its armoured body. Emerging from its hiding place, the robot pounded the floor like a gorilla; its three huge mechanical arms it used to walk upon rocked the floor as it lurched forward. It's body encased in white armour supporting a partial lower spherical body off the floor with no legs to mention of, even so it must have stood easily over 15feet like a robotic Behemoth. From the top of the curved body arose an angular head with three cameras, scanning the commotion like glowing blood red eyes as the bullets sparked and bounced off its exterior. Raising a hand again, it swept another hard blow, this time taking two of the security guards down as it began to lower its body to the floor and rest. Its head sank back into the recess in the body and its arms locked against itself transforming into a perfectly white seamless sphere. The huge ball began to roll forward down one of the corridors gaining a fast pace quickly as it ran down the staff members in its way, leaving red streaks across its white, bullet marked armour as the weight of the metal beast which must easily weighed over five tons, squashed its victims in to the floor and against walls leaving nothing but a twitching mess in its trail. From back in the lift more footsteps could be heard walking across the metal floor out into the open.

Jodie stared from the doorway in horror as the remaining members of security swapped gun magazines ready to open fire on the second wave of robot creatures. These stood about 7feet tall and were more humanoid in their design. They slowly walked over to each member of the team,

Doppelganger

Medical droid from Hell

Exo-Skeleton before

this thing still gives me nightmares

their bodies were a white and grey mechanical skeleton with white armour but not the same as the first behemoth that just rolled away. The bullets had more effect on these, but not enough to stop them completely. They hobbled, broken from the gun blasts, like shuffling zombies toward each member of security, forcing them back against the wall. Still Jodie watched on as the lumbering mechanical bodies walked on taking damage but never stopping as they reached their targets. Grasping one of the guards by the throat, one of the robots lifted its victim up against the wall, staring at him with its broken face plate as if to wonder what the strange thing was it had caught. The guard looked on, terrified at the faceless creature and in his fear and frustration screamed. The robots dented and broken face armour began to twist and rearrange itself until it had formed the guards face upon its mangled bullet damaged armour like a grotesque doppelganger of the original. Where the robot's hands gripped the man it began to change. Its white armour began to analyse and mimic anything it was near to. The lower arm which pinned the man's gun and hand, started to form a weapons barrel and ammunition clip while the arm holding its prey's throat also began to change colour as the blood from the man's neck ran down the robots arm, the sharp metal on its fingers had cut into the man's skin which started to cause the robots armour to turn red as it mimicked everything it sampled. The robot disarmed the man by crushing his hand so he could no longer hold the weapon. The robot then extended its arm out. It raised its hand to the man's face as its fingers started to twist and unfold growing thinner and sharper like knifes. With great speed it released a fine thread, the equivalent to a spiders webbing through its pointed fingers and sewed the man's mouth shut. Reaching down again, it slowly pressed its finger blades through his stomach as the man writhed in agony, unable to make a louder noise above a murmur as he slowly lost consciousness through the pain to its inevitable outcome. The other robots had also executed the other guards around the room and taken on the form of their victims' bodies which were now silent except from the odd moans from the severely injured or dying. Leaning down the new robots picked any weapons and split up to cover the different hallways, one of them leading straight towards Jodie's hiding place. Jodie began to panic as the mutated shaped robot staggered up the corridor, blasting with its gun shaped armour at any survivor still moving. Checking around the corner again the robot had drawn nearer toward the room she was hiding in. In the other direction was safety, at least safety from what was about to find her. The robot lumbered forward treading on and over bodies as it surveyed the scene, now only a few feet away from the doorway. Jodie could see the skeletal shadow upon the door creeping closer, she pinned herself against the wall as the sweat from her brow began to roll down her face in fear, she struggled to control her breathing so as not to give herself away. The robot stumbled and reached out with its hand to steady itself, the impact rocked the wall she stood against. She felt the fingers drag along the wall just the other side of her. She closed her eyes for just a second only to open them to see the sharp metal hand reach around the door frame, crushing it in its powerful grip. She desperately looked around for an escape but there was nothing. The whole room was within a complex and didn't even have a window to use, what chance did she have against the inhuman creature if guns and body armour could not stop it. She held her breath and prepared herself to make a run for it. It might not get her far but it was the one thing she knew she could do, the metal hand pulled on the wall damaging it further as she braced herself, and ran.

Why would you create this?

I know its Medical use, but its creepy as hell.

Chapter 4
Déjà vu again!

Racing through the door Jodie caught the doppelganger robot off guard and it reeled backwards to take in the new information. Looking back over her shoulder she caught sight of the robot taking aim as it corrected its posture. Looking ahead she was already half way up the hallway to safety. The robot moved its feet to counter the recoil, as it did so a survivor awoke from the Behemoth attack, not knowing the new robot was there he tried to reach out and crawl with his half crushed body. The robot's foot came down on the man's arm, causing it to lose balance as it fired off a shot from its arm shotgun, which it had formed from the security weapons. The blast blew a hole in the wall to the side of Jodie's head, she gave out a quick scream while she continued running. The robot steadied itself and looked down at its new obstacle. Aiming down to the sound of screaming from the man it was standing on, it fired off several blasts into its helpless victim. Raising its head it scanned the corridor ahead looking for its first target which had now disappeared out of view. The robot lowered its weapon and continued its sweep of the immediate area.

Jodie gasped for breath as she grabbed her side with stitch, staggering onward in case the doppelganger was still in pursuit. In a daze of panic she made her way through the corridors heading to the main doors to make her escape, in the background the echo of single gunshots rang through the air as the robots found any member of staff trapped within the offices and executed them on sight. Corner after corner she turned, the pain in her side now easing as her pace slowed to a fast walk. Up ahead was the security door, which led back into the main complex, a smile began to form but just a little too soon for celebration. THUD after loud THUD came down the corridor behind her, but it wasn't gun shots this time. Walking back to the junction of the corridor she peered around in the direction the noise was coming from. From far back in the dim lights she could see movement. A huge white metallic ball rolled toward her, each loud thud was bouncing of the walls. Jodie turned and ran for the security doors, grabbing for her swipe card in her lab coat pocket. The huge door was all that stood in her way as she swiped her pass. From around the corner the huge Behemoth sphere rolled into sight, sensing a target its internal gyroscope whirred faster as it began to gain speed. The doors unlocked and Jodie grabbed the handle and pulled with all her strength in the hope it would help to make enough space for her to get through quickly. Closer the armoured sphere came, bouncing and crashing off the walls as Jodie jumped through the door in the nick of time. The Behemoth hit the other side of the door shutting it tight, causing a large dent in the metal. Jodie was caught by the impact, breaking her left arm as she passed through the gap in the door and was sent flying across the shiny tiles landing badly on the floor and in pain. Sliding to a halt Jodie gripped her arm tight as another THUD came from the door as it tried to break through it. She staggered to her feet and moved away as fast as she could. Turning a corner she looked back at the metal door, slowly bending with the weight of each impact, not looking where she was running.

"LOOK OUT" shouted a man's voice as the two collided and knocked each other down. Jodie screamed in pain jarring her arm and fought to open her eyes to see what had happened.

Across from her was a security guard who had also been knocked to the floor. The man climbed to his feet, placed his gun strap over his shoulder and extended his hand out to help.

"Hello, are you ok? Do you understand me?" he asked with a calm voice. "Miss, are you hurt, can I help you" he asked again.

Jodie stared up at him in shock and also relief "Yes, yes" she answered and reached out to grab his open hand, which gave her a static shock as their fingers met with a strange orange spark as he pulled her to her feet again.

Jodie shook off the shock then pointed to where the pain was, "it's my arm, I think it's broken."

The guard checked her arm for the break and motioned to her to remove her lab coat. Taking it slow, she removed the coat sleeve from her arm. The guard pulled a knife to cut and rip at the coat so he could wrap it around Jodie's shoulder to make a sling.

"Could be a fracture, broken on one side but not all the way, you'll be ok. There we go, how's it feel?" he asked.

"Good" she replied "and, thank you."

"Nice outfit, always wear that to work" laughed the man. "Shall we get back to the others?" he asked.

"I've just come from a party, it would have been fine under the coat, although that doesn't matter now anyway. Others? How many made it to here?" questioned Jodie.

"I was just doing a final sweep before heading back to the lobby, where those that have made it have regrouped, when I came across you, quite lucky really as we're about to lock this place down tight" and he smiled as if to reassure her everything was going to be ok. This seemed to set her at ease as they walked together toward the security doors.

"I'm Jodie, by the way and thank you" she smiled at the guard "you even seem to have scared away the robot at the door, I cant hear him anymore."

"Yeah, I seem to have that effect, probably why they hired me" he replied with a small laugh under his breath. The guard stopped and turned extending his hand out to shake hers.

"Sorry where are my manners, I'm security patrol 32, or you could just call me Hobs."

Walking on they came to the to the lobby door where they could see the

27

people gathered on the other side. Hobs knocked at the glass "OPEN UP" he shouted.

Jodie laughed "How long have you worked here again? You do know that's sound proof so they can't hear you."

Hobs smiled "Oh! Well that explains a lot, I just thought they were deaf or getting old or something," he joked with a cough as he tried to hide his embarrassment looking around as if searching for something.

Jodie laughed again, "Not to worry, I've still got my pass so I can swipe through." As she began to search her pockets with her good right arm, patting down any available place where it might be.

"Something wrong" asked Hobs?

"My pass, I can't find it. I must have lost it back at the last door, I'll have to go back" sighed Jodie.

Hobs readied his gun which was strapped over his shoulder "Come on then let's go."

Jodie stopped him, "It's not that far back I'm sure I know where it will be, I can just nip back and get it now the coast it clear."

"Fine" he replied "but I'll be at the end of this corridor on lookout if you need me."

"Ooh! My hero" she grinned, Hobs just smiled as she walked back.

Back at the security door Jodie looked around where she had fallen for the missing pass. The thick metal of the door was dented from the impact of the behemoth's attack. She began to look under cupboards and behind the odd plant pot for where it could have landed when she was thrown. From within one of the rooms she heard a shuffle from something moving within. The lights were not on and the door was ajar. Again there came another shuffle and clatter of items falling over. Looking around she searched for anything to be used as a weapon. By the side of an office was the caretakers mop and bucket, carefully she crept over and took the mop out which dripped all over the floor. Placing her foot on the mop end she pulled hard with her one good arm until the handle came loose, the exertion sent pain through her broken arm causing her to let out a small yell of pain regardless of how hard she tried not too. Taking the mop handle in hand, she made her way toward the door where the noise had come from. Slowly she pushed open the door with the handle, ready for whatever might be in there. Jodie stared into the darkened room turning to check the corners before she edged forward. From in the back corner of the room came glowing circles of light, which blinked at Jodie as she starred at what seemed to be eyes looking at her? The eyes blinked again and fell to the floor, once again looking back. With the sound of tiny foot steps the eyes came closer before appearing into the light, it was a black cat.

Jodie was taken by surprise; all the weeks working at the facility she had never encountered a single animal. The cat walked over and sat by her feet, just staring but with an almost human mannerisms and a long lost feeling of friends that had been reunited. Kneeling to the floor she placed the mop handle down and tapped her knee for the cat to come closer. Before she could finish the cat jumped up and instantly began to purr and rub it's head against Jodie. If anyone could have seen it they would have thought that her own cat had come to greet her. Jodie fussed at the cat, stroking from head to tail, the cat purred louder and lifted to rub its head against her face and lick at her cheek.

"Well aren't you friendly" smiled Jodie "I don't suppose you have seen my pass card on your travels eh little kitty?"

The cat stopped as if to listen, then jumped from her knee and began to look around.

"You're a strange little cat, what are you up to now?"

The cat glanced over as Jodie spoke but continued on in its search before stopping at a nearby doorway. Reaching out with its claws it began to scratch and pull, Jodie raised to her feet to get a better look at the cat, thinking it had gone crazy. The cat continued to scratch until something

Strange to
see a cat?

Where did it
come from or
how did it get
in here?

seemed to appear from the gap under the door. Stopping and sitting straight up the cat looked over to Jodie and just for a split second, she thought it motioned to her with its head to come over to it. Shrugging this off as the pain in her arm making her see things, she walked over to see what it had found. Looking at the doorway where the cat sat, Jodie saw the photo on her pass sticking out; it must have slid under when she was hit. Picking the pass up and placing it in her pocket, Jodie then put her arm around the cat and lifted it up to her face.

"Thanks so much for your help" and she pressed her nose against the cats head, the cat did the same and purred again. From around the corner came Hobs voice, his footsteps echoing down the hallway "JODIE, YOU OK" he shouted with concern in his tone. As Jodie turned in his direction, the cat gave out a hiss and leapt from her knee scratching her right hand with its claws as it leapt to the floor, the hair on its back and tail standing on end as it gave another hiss toward the corridor and ran away.

Hobs appeared around the corner "There you are, I was getting worried, did you find it?"

Jodie got to her feet and got out the card, "Yeah got it" and flashed it at him with her small bloodied scratch dripping from the back of her hand.

"How do you get those scratches" he asked, "Is everything alright" he quizzed Jodie.

"Yes, yeah, it's fine, the card had slipped under the door and there must have been a nail or rough patch that caught my hand when I got it" she lied to his face deciding the cat encounter was a story too crazy to explain, "Lets get back then shall we" she asked "Its weird, but, I just get the feeling I've done this all before" she added as she smiled at him and gave one last glance down the corridor to where the cat ran off. Hobs just nodded as she passed him noticing the direction she was looking. His expression changed as he didn't believe one word she had just said.

"Yeah, we need to get you back so someone can check your arm out" he replied, giving one last visual sweep of the area she had looked toward. Jodie walked away and Hobs turned around as the two set off back to the lobby. From within a broken air vent the cat reappeared, constantly looking in the direction the two had just walked. With a low growl the cat looked on. Checking the coast was clear, it gave out a loud meow and turned away to venture further into the facility with a tiny patter of paws down the corridor.

Had round glasses

Dr Lockwood

Chapter 5
Cause and effect

Jodie and Hobs passed through into the lobby area, there were very few people, maybe a dozen staff and a further eight security left. Jodie ran to the entrance, the huge security shutters had closed when the alarms went off, Jodie began to pound at them with her good arm.

Pete, the head guard, came over to her.

"It's no use Jodie we're trapped, until this thing is over we aren't going anywhere. Best we can do is wait for backup to come and help us."

"Great" she replied, "how long is that going to take."

"Who knows" he replied "this has never happened before, I don't even know what the back up is or if the alarm registered a call, if it didn't then we could be here for a few days until they realise there's a problem, apart from the killer robots there's plenty of supplies."

Jodie turned her back to the door and slid down to the floor with a huff.

Hobs came over to where they were "Is there access to the cameras anywhere so we can check what's going on?"

"No, all access to security is restricted to a team on one of the lower levels, the control centre is back in there" replied Pete pointing to the security doors they had just come through.

"What about medical supplies" asked Jodie "do we have anything for the pain in my arm?"

Pete nodded, "Sure thing, I have a kit with supplies under the desk, I'll get it for you, see if there's anything you can take."

While Jodie went over to sort out the kit with Pete, Hobs went to speak to the other security guards, a few seemed to be from the lower levels and might know more about what was going on.

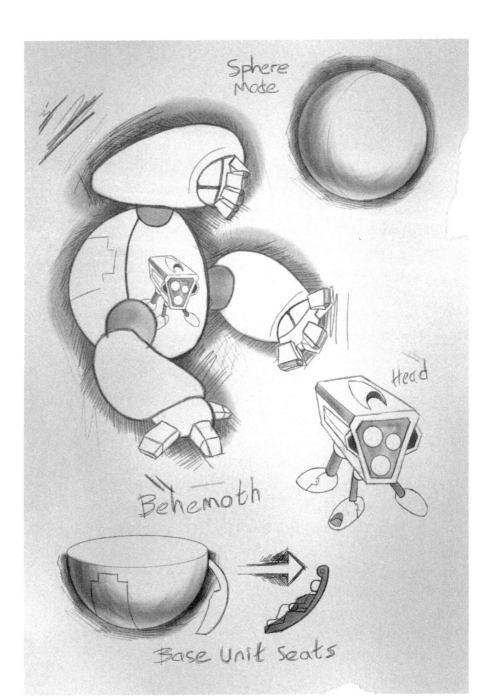

Sphere Mode

Head

Behemoth

Base Unit Seats

It was an hour before Jodie met up with Hobs again.

"How's the arm holding up" he asked as he passed her a bottle of water.

"Better now I've taken something for it, thanks for the drink."

She adjusted the make shift sling.

"I've spoken to the other security guards and they seem to agree that power from the shard did this, somehow?" said Hobs.

Jodie agreed "Yeah, this all started the moment of that power surge. So how do we reverse it?"

From one of the huddles of scientists a voice spoke up, "I might be able to help you."

A man with a short slim build, scruffy hair about late 20's with round spectacles in a lab coat raised his hand to get their attention. "I'm Dr Lockwood, I'm new here but I was stationed on the lower levels with Dr Williams for most of my stay where we worked on the shard. If you could find me a laptop and a few tools I might be able to hack the system and show you a way of draining the shards energy."

Hobs questioned the scientist with a hint of scepticism "Will this stop what's happening?"

The doctor squirmed in the shadow of the tall guard "Maybe, I'm not sure, but it's happened before" he answered sheepishly. Hobs shouted to the entire room "SOMEONE GET THIS MAN A LAPTOP AND SET OF TOOLS NOW."

As the staff members searched for the equipment Jodie approached the doctor "those robots, those things that are killing everyone, do you know what they are?"

The doctor stopped his search and turned to explain what he knew.

"This may come as a surprise but firstly; the bigger robot with three arms was built for search and rescue. The whole idea behind it was it could traverse any terrain; either at speed as a sphere where it needed to it could walk with its three large arms. As you've already seen it's strong and smart enough to meet any demands, anything else it can smash through, dig out or climb up, so its best not to get in its way, because if it wants in anywhere, it's only a matter of time. As a tripod it's quite slow and lumbering but is incredibly strong, upon reaching its extraction target it can encase itself into a sphere and transport three people within its body. The inner robot at this point detaches from its white armour which is a diamond hard armoured shell, while its inner body stays upright in one position using its weight shift for steering. The shell is rotated through magnetism, much like the way a bullet train hovers above its track but in this case it's the body within a shell, this method also helps ensure that its passengers dont get sick by not constantly spinning them. I was able to test ride in it and to be fair its about as smooth as riding on a train, but in the wrong hands this is basically a tank that can think. On the plus side, this facility could only afford to create one working prototype but it's heavily armoured and as a sphere it's completely impenetrable not to mention, given enough room, it can pick up a lot of speed. Personally I've no idea how you might be able to stop this hulking Behemoth, it's built to withstand a direct missile strike. Best I can say is if you see it, pray it doesn't see you and hide, unless you have two missiles handy."

"The second more humanoid looking is, surprisingly, a medical droid. It's main under body is tall and built like a human skeleton but it's the white armour surrounding it that's the interesting part. It's armour isn't really there for protection even though it is able to absorb small arms fire. Upon finding a patient it scans the targets body, assess the injury and through electrical pulses creates a new body part from its armour. You see the armour is hundreds of tiny biological robots that can be programmed to mimic a shape, cells, bones even minerals from basic commands from the main body. This armour is already in a basic body shape much in the same vain as a shop mannequin, to adjust faster to a patients medical needs, so let's say for example you're a soldier and your thigh has been blown off in an explosion. The robot can scan the person's leg area to assess original shape and muscle mass, it then sends pulses to its leg armour which alters to match the victims. This then detaches like a thick top skin and is placed upon the wounded area. Initially the new body part shell acts like a bandage on the patient. Then it begins to fuse into the skin and multiply using the blood supply as a catalyst to duplicate, like dividing cells until it itself becomes the missing part of the leg, replacing skin and bone and even replicating skin tone. The initial contact stabilises the wound and then the whole process takes several hours to complete, then over the healing period the tiny bio-bots will merge with the body's DNA as the accelerated skin regeneration takes place until the leg is completely restored. The same goes for the arms, chest and even the face. Although we haven't quite yet develop an eye or any other more complex organs, bone and skin are an amazing achievement. Imagine breaking your arm then having its full use restored by the next day. The robot's remaining white bio- armour can also regenerate, so it can continue to help multiple casualties, If you want to damage this model, the quickest method will be to aim for the main robot skeleton as it can't repair itself, unless of course it figures out how to replicate parts from its bio-armour? Its possible if it's replicating weapons, so the best bet would be to knock it down and remove the head. You might have noticed that they are scanning their victims and replicating how they look but not removing the armour, makes them look like some kind of robotic mannequin zombie, just creepy. As you may have seen its hands are equipped for surgery should the situation require it, unfortunately it's also been using these tools as weapons. Overall, easier to take down but harder to keep down, just don't get within its reach or let it grab anything dangerous it can mimic as it is equipped to be the perfect Doppelganger."

Approaching from the side a few of the other scientist and technicians brought over the equipment and tools they had found. Lockwood set to work and rigged up the laptop to the network, removing panels and stripping wires to create a connection. As he logged on to the system Jodie, Hobs and a few others gathered around.

With insanely fast typing the doctor began to hack into the facilities security system "So firstly let me get into the secure lab recordings," with the clatter of the keyboard keys he brought up the video log. With a crackle the video began to play, it was Dr Williams with his usual dry stony faced demeanour.

'This is video log, quote reference 6-24-6 for archiving purposes. Today we are continuing to try to measure the shard's energy. In previous experiments, due to unforeseen side effects, we have failed to identify what units of energy it emits as it is more powerful than any other currently recorded. To my side you can clearly see what looks like a small rotating blue swirl or portal as we're calling it, as it has no apparent depth greater to its physical size but we have found it to be able to hold any object that passes through it. This appeared during initial tests whilst trying to channel an electrical pulse through the shard. It somehow used this power and fired out a short burst of energy which in turn caused the portal to appear. To note, one of the assistants measuring how deep the anomaly was passed a two metre pipe into it. Unfortunately some kind of suction pulled the pipe in at great speed along with the assistant's arm. This was torn off at the shoulder, we believe from something on the other side which left claw marks in the remaining skin tissue. Sadly we were unable to retrieve the pipe, but we wish the assistant a speedy recovery and good luck in his new career which he seems to be adapting to single handed. He has been replaced for this session by Dr Lockwood whom you can see behind me. To begin this session we are trying to take a smaller fragment for examination to see if there is any reaction to a piece of it being separated from the main body of the shard. Before this session started we carefully took a thin slice from the end of the shard and placed it in this airtight transparent containment box. Now if Dr Lockwood would do the honours we will see what happens when we move the slice near to the portal. The procedure for cutting the shard was completed in a sealed environment in case there was any loss of the unidentified energy. As you can see the slice is glowing with an orange hue or mist around it and seems to be attracted to Dr Lockwood's hand as he carries the case. The case now stands against the portal and the doctor's hands are now away from it. We can see the mist energy has reached out from the slice rather like an appendage of some kind or tentacle might be a better explanation, toward the portal. Now if we can see what happens when we open the secure case, doctor, if you please? As you can see the orange energy has connected to the portal and is slowly being absorbed, as a side effect the portal seems to be increasing in size. I can now walk over to the open case and see that the slice is now completely dark, lifeless, devoid of power and nothing more than a crystallized ember. Experiment over and now to test for further results.'

The video stopped and Lockwood looked around at the others who just stared in wonder.
"What this shows" he began to explain, "is that, whatever that blue swirl is, it will absorb anything, even the power out of that shard."
Hobs spoke up first "So if we can get hold of the shard in the main lab which is now unsecured and find one of those blue portal things we can possibly bring an end to all this?"
"Great" said Jodie "let's do that so we can get out of here."
Pete was the next to speak up. "There's just one problem, the shard is back through the security doors where those things are and we don't have a blue spinning portal to put it in."

41

Lockwood paused for a second before answering "That's not quite true, we do actually have the same portal in one of the lower levels."

Typing away again at the laptop the doctor bought up security camera control and loaded up one of the secure camera feeds. "Here it is," he said as he pointed to the live screen footage.

"Using a magnetic cage we were able to move the portal to a lower level. It had to go in the biggest area we had because as soon as you put a power source near to it, it would grow. It was moved three times to larger rooms before we realised it was draining energy from the computers."

Jodie stared at the portal on screen "So instead of a six inch portal of spinning blue stuff you now have a six foot portal that can drain energy, nice going, instead of an arm you can now lose an entire person."

"I know" said the doctor, "several staff that worked in the room have gone missing, we were unable to find any of them."

Pete spoke up from the awkward silence "To save waiting here to be rescued how about we make a move of our own."

Hobs nodded in agreement "Pete, I want you here with two other security to look after Dr Lockwood and his friends who will provide guidance from the hacked camera system once we get to the shard room. As the higher ranked here, myself and the other four guards will head into the facility to retrieve the shard and get it through the portal in the hope it will reverse this entire mess we're in. Jodie stay here with the doctor and Pete."

The newly formed team led by Hobs equipped themselves with weapons from a security locker, anything they could carry before setting off to the main doors.

Chapter 6
The Ember Shard

The science crew with Jodie and Pete watched the screen using the hacked security feed to follow Hobs and his team.

Hobs radioed in to Pete, "Ok, we're going to head toward the second security door."

Jodie watched as the team moved from one corridor to the next, checking every corner, whilst Dr Lockwood used the camera feeds to check for danger ahead of them. Turning the last corner the second large door stood before them, bowed from the weight of the behemoth blows when it tried to break through after Jodie. Hobs signalled to one of the guards to check it out while the others covered all entry points in case any stray robots appeared that were trapped after the door was shut. The first guard by the door signalled over to Hobs who went to inspect the door. Hobs walked to the centre of the room where the camera feed was and spoke over the radio to Lockwood.

"This doors taken a battering, don't think its going to open, do you know of another way in doctor?"

"Yes, its possible I can get you in but you'll need my pass to get through it" replied Lockwood.

Jodie spoke up "I'll take it, I know my way around the main floor level, plus delivery is mainly what I did so I can get there in no time."

Pete put his hand on her shoulder "You can't go Jodie your unarmed and injured."

Jodie just shrugged him off "Its fine, I can get there quickly, my arm is ok at the moment plus the fact they just swept the area and found nothing. I'm also the most expendable member here and I know this area better than anyone else, you and the other two need to stay here to protect the scientists and they need to stay here in case we need advice when we reach the lower labs."

Before Pete could agree Jodie had grabbed Lockwood's card and swiped though the first security door.

"Stay there Hobs, Jodie is on her way with the pass, please confirm when she reaches you" said Pete over the radio, Hobs just waved to the camera in acknowledgement.

As the door shut behind her Jodie made her way through the facility. It was all strangely quiet. The stark white corridors were usually full of people under the bright lighting, but now everything turned grey in the broken lights as smashed florescent tubes crunched underfoot every once in a while. Corridor after corridor was the same, silent, full of stray documents, papers dropped and trodden upon the floor, broken glass, overturned cabinets and desks. It was now just a short walk to the second door where Hobs was waiting. She was sure she could hear the echo's of them talking up ahead as she passed by the empty offices when the strangest sight appeared before her. A golden glowing orb emerged through the wall, floating softly like a bubble in a breeze, swaying this way and that. Jodie became curious and followed it and tried to get closer as it appeared like it would pass through a nearby office door. SMASH went the door toward her as a huge fist burst through the wood grabbing at the glowing orb which quickly zoomed away out of sight. Jodie dodged the blow, slipping to the floor in panic and fear, gritting her teeth from the pain in her arm. Looking up, the huge bulk of a Doppelganger peered out the doorway, its twisted face in the shape of some poor victim it had tried to copy. Jodie scrabbled back to her feet in a panic as the huge robotic arm grabbed out at her. Escaping to the side, she began to run back the way she had come, the robot close behind her. Turning a corner she came across the black cat from earlier standing next to a large open vent, it gave a loud meow. With the thuds of the robot getting nearer, Jodie ran over to the cat and slid across the floor into the vent to hide, her teeth gritted in pain from the jolt to her arm. The cat ran off up the corridor leaving Jodie to wait, nursing her arm. The thuds drew closer as the robot searched, shaking the floor where Jodie was hiding. Unseen to her, she could hear the cat beginning to meow loudly, which caught the robots attention. Stomping past Jodie's hiding place the robot pursued its new target. Shuffling forward slowly, being careful of her arm she caught the last glimpse of the robot going around the corner and out of sight. Jodie got to her feet, she heard the loud crackle as a bright light lit up the corridor where the robot had gone. Another followed, then another as the lights changed colours and she heard a loud bang of metal hitting the floor. Slowly curiosity got the better of her and she crept up to the corner to look around. Taking a deep breath she popped her head around to a bizarre view, the Doppelganger was lifeless facedown upon the floor, on its back was the black cat which gave another loud 'MEOW,' turned and ran away.

The sound of heavy boots stomped down the corridor as Hobs and his team ran to Jodie after hearing the fighting. Turning around the last bend they were shocked to see Jodie standing over the fallen robot.

Hobs walked over to her while the others stood guard "Are you ok, what happened?"

Jodie didn't know what to say "I don't know, it came after me, I ran and slid down into the vent around the corner. I saw it walk past me around to here and there was this noise and light. By the time I crawled out I found it like this, that's when you appeared."

Hobs inspected the robots armour, it was scalded and blackened with several visible marks that he could see, "I've seen these kind of scald marks before, years ago, Jodie, are you sure there is nothing else you saw or want to tell me?"

Jodie just shook her head as she changed the subject "I have the pass you need for the door, shall we go get this crystal thingy" and off she walked. Hobs stared as she walked away, his face showed he just didn't believe that was the whole truth.

"Come on, hurry up" she shouted to the team as she headed for the security door.

Hobs caught up to Jodie and passed her his gun. This is a UMP45 or as you might know it, a submachine gun. This is mine but I'm still going to show you the basics just in case. I don't want you walking around here unable to defend yourself should the need arise. Hobs quickly went through the uses of the weapon, from firing to reloading. Taking his revolver from his holster he passed it to Jodie.

"This is a MP412.Rex a Russian made revolver. The main difference with this is unlike most barrel loading weapons that push out to the side like you see in the movies, this one folds forward. It pushes the empty shells out of the chambers to give you a faster reload. I don't think these ever went into full production, I had to go to Hell and back to find one but that's another story. So here it is and while you're in my company its all yours, lets load it up and give it a test so you know what to expect in case you need to use it."

Jodie took the heavy gun in her right hand, adjusting her grip and feeling a little nervous yet excited at the same time having never held any kind of weapon before. Hobs pointed out an upright folder down the far end of the corridor upon a cabinet.

"There's your target about 30 metres, lets see how good a shot you are." He took a step back to clear the way for her shot. Jodie raised the gun with a slight shake of her hand and took aim. Hobs spoke softly behind her so not to cause a distraction. "Keep both eyes on the target, when your ready just exhale as you squeeze the trigger, stay calm and in your own tim....."

Bang, went the gun cutting Hobs sentence short. Jodie lowered the weapon with a big smile on her face.

"Wow, that was fun" she beamed.

Hobs walked with Jodie over to the folder and picked it up off the floor

"I don't think we're going to have a problem here, you're a natural, dead centre."

Back at the door the team could once again be seen on camera in the lobby. Hobs radioed in for new instructions from Lockwood.

"Ok Hobs, take my card from Jodie and swipe at the keypad located to the right of the main door. Once you've done this a hidden panel should open next to it, punch in the number 7867546, remember this for later to get into the lab. If you look at the key pad it's in the same layout as a mobile phone so just remember the number spells pumpkin."

"Very apt given today's date" murmured Hobs to Jodie who smiled at his quip.

"Ok doctor what next" but Hobs question was already answered.

The huge door began to make a noise of bolts and levers adjusting, then from above and to the sides of their position the noise grew. Down the centre of the structure the main surrounding wall began to open up and slide apart making the attached dented security door look like a small access hatch. The two halves split and began to move to either side in an impressive display of mechanical engineering. The team and Jodie stood ready to enter the unlocked area to get to the lift then down to the labs. Suddenly from between the doors stretched out a large robotic hand which turned slowly and rather menacingly as it took aim and opened fire. The hail of bullets from its arm mounted gun tore the first guards head to shreds, every bullet a direct hit. The team scattered for cover as the doors opened further and a group of three doppelgangers forced their way through with the lead robot opening fire on the remaining team. Hobs gave the orders.

"Team, take out the main robot, the others are unarmed but still dangerous, DO NOT allow any of them to take hold of a gun."

The four of them returned fire, slowly cutting away at the robot's armour forcing it down to its knees. As the team fired at the main target the two other robots spread out, their razor sharp fingers outstretched and ready

47

to strike. In the ensuing gun battle the first robot fell, its body riddled with holes and dents from the security teams bullets who were now having to reload. One of the Doppelgangers took a swipe at the closest guard who defended himself using the empty UMP45 to block the blow. The razor fingers sliced through the metal of the gun and the bones of the guard's hand. Screaming in agony he held what was left of his hand by the wrist as his scream was cut short by a second blow from his attacker across his throat taking his head off with a single swipe. Around the room the others had reloaded as Hobs and the two remaining guards reopened fire on the two other robots, one was heading to Hobs and the other toward the other two guards. Hobs emptied his gun into the body and head of the grotesque robot whose armour had moulded into the misshapen semblance of a mutilated member of the staff. As he went to reload the Doppelganger pulled back its arm and punched out at Hobs with its finger blades extended out toward his face. With a quick duck and a roll Hobs missed the blow but was caught by the following arm which swung around hitting him sending him sliding across the floor in one direction and his gun and clip in another. The robot lunged forward and arched itself over the unarmed Hobs, its arm pulled back ready to strike. With a volley of bullets to its head, Hobs looked on as the hot metal tore through the robots neck until its head fell off, catching it in his hands. He looked up at Jodie, who now held an empty machine gun which was smoking in her hand.

"Bet-cha glad you taught me the basics eh?" she asked.

Climbing to his feet Hobs took his gun back and turned with Jodie to see that the two other guards had taken care of the surviving robot. Stripping the two dead team members of ammo and anything else of use the remaining team ran off through the doors toward the elevators where the first encounter had taken place. Stepping through the bloodied mess they entered the lift through the broken doors and went down to the lower level.

Chapter 7
Destiny

The now three man team entered the unlocked lab. Each took position to secure the room while Jodie waited for them to finish before following. The lab was a mess with broken equipment and squashed body parts. At the centre of the room was the main experiment area where Dr Williams had been standing during the video broadcast. The red mush on the floor was all that was left after the attack. Hobs reset the main camera and checked in with Lockwood and Pete who were still watching in the lobby. Hobs took position by the main camera to form a triangle of cover between the other guards. Shouting to Jodie, Hobs asked her to come over to him as he pushed aside the debris to reveal the shard lying on the floor, gripped tightly by the burnt disembodied hand of Dr Williams. "Jodie, as we are covering you at the moment can you please pick up the shard so we can get out of here" asked Hobs a little nervously while keeping a tight check on the two main doors within the room.

Jodie walked over with a slip and a squelch under her feet from the blood and chunks of flesh that were strewn over the floor. Kneeling down she held out her hand to pick up the shard before pausing, "Its ok to touch this thing isn't it, I mean, after all it's caused." Hobs nodded and smiled as a bead of sweat passed over his forehead. "Yeah, should be fine" and motioned to her to pick it up.

Reaching out again she quickly snatched up the shard and shook it until the fingers were loose enough to drop the hand back on to the floor with a squelch. She held it in her hand as it began to give off a brighter glow, then she tucked it into her sling pulling the revolver back out to make room. Hobs watched on intensely, noticing the shards reaction to her and without the effect it had on the last person who handled it years before.

Hobs signalled for them to all advance and called into the lobby, "Lockwood, Pete, we've got the shard and we're moving on to the lower security room to the portal."

Lockwood replied back, "Its plain sailing from here in, except for the robots I mean. The portal room has been removed of most power sources except for basic lighting. Follow the corridors further into the complex, if you come to a junction, just look for which has the least cables running to it, should take you straight there."

Hobs seemed to pause taking in the information while scanning the ceiling for cables,

"Roger that information, so is there anything else we need from you now Doc?"

Lockwood's voice came over a crackling radio,

"As long as you're careful that's pretty much everything from us."

"Thanks for the guide, we'll go and get the job finished." Spoke Hobs as he murmured "Adios doc."

Back in the lobby Lockwood and Pete watched as Jodie and the other guards walked away leaving Hobs just staring at the camera. Pete points to the screen,

"What's the matter with him, he lost something."

Lockwood turns and watches,

"Yeah, I'll give him a call see what he wants."

Before the doctor could speak over the radio there came a loud bang at the door. The whole room paused in a sudden intake of breath. Another bang came at the door as it began to buckle under the weight of the impact. Everyone took a step back as Pete and the remaining lobby guards readied their guns. A third loud bang came from the door, this time causing a gap between it and the wall. Movement and flashes of silver, metal and white could be seen as three large metal fingers pushed through the gap and in a show of power peeled the thick security door

slowly off the wall. The Behemoth pushed its way in and swung the door like a Frisbee across the room crushing its first victim under its weight. Pounding its fist in to the floor it made its way to the centre of the lobby as Pete and his team opened fire. The shots bounced off harmlessly as it began to swing it great arms to smash anyone within its reach. From its half sphere belly three hatches opened up revealing seating areas, much like a scaled down pilots chair and in each seat was the curled up body of a Doppelganger. Each one dropped to the floor and began to unfurl its limbs, their twisted armour mimicking that of it's last victim as they set off to acquire more. One of the scientists worked his way around the back walls in an attempt to escape out the open door. Creeping his way to safety he turned into the path of another oncoming Doppelganger, its spindly blade like fingers twitching and tapping together. It placed its white blank head face to face with the man and with a spark of energy transformed to resemble him silently screaming back at him. The man's face changed as he looked down, the finger blades from the Doppelgangers hand firmly within his stomach. As his strength faded his body slid off and crumpled to the floor. The Doppelganger clenched its red fingers then turned its gaze to the lobby. Over by the video link Lockwood grabbed the laptop and crawled under the desk with the radio in hand. Before he could do anything else a set of sharp razor claws pierced the desk and slowly dragged through the wood toward him. He looked on in fear at what would be his death. To the side of the lobby, a bloodied and beaten Pete saw the doctor's end and charged at the Doppelganger, shots from his gun ringing out as bullet after bullet hit the robot creatures face, knocking it to the floor. Pete grabbed the radio to get a message to the others,

"Hobs, Jodie, ANYONE. The lobby is lost, we've been over run, our only chance is to make a break for......"

Pete's last words failed him as the sharp finger blades passed through his back into his lungs and out through his chest as easy as a hot knife through butter, as the bullet ridden head of the robot slowly appeared over his shoulder as if to gloat at its handy work. As Pete sat on the floor dying he looked to the laptop, Hobs was still standing staring at the camera, it was the last thing Pete saw before his vision faded to black. The robot swiped its hand up and out casting the body away, then it to gazed at the laptop and scanned the live link for the location of the others still alive within the facility. The robot stared back at the screen as the image of Hobs turned and walked away. With a crackle of orange power fizzing through its circuits it pulled away. Raising to its feet it started to walk toward the door, the other robots turned and followed, the sound of their foot steps was all that was left as the lobby fell silent.

Back on the lower level Jodie was running to find Hobs.
"Did you hear Pete, DID YOU? What's going on tell me," her fist banging on Hobs chest in frustration and panic.
Hobs reached up and grabbed her arm and stared back, gently shaking his head.
"I'm sorry Jodie, they're all gone, it's just us now and I suspect they know that and will be on their way for us. Team, find a defensive position and expect company."
The four of them moved along the corridors until they found a clear lab where Hobs gave the orders.
"We'll hold up here, the re-enforced doors and walls were built to withstand and contain a large blast should any experiment go wrong so it should help against them battering their way in and also help channel them single file so we have more of a chance of hitting them together. I expect a search party first as they wont know where we are. We get rid of them, then on my signal move to the next position, make it difficult for them to find us."
The team set to work securing the three lab doors and closed any shutters over the viewing area windows and settled in for a fight, each covering a

door with Jodie in the middle holding her gun and securing the shard within her sling, but they didn't have long to wait.

The first guard shouts over "Movement in the corridor, two of them moving this way sir."

The Doppelgangers caught sight of their prey and quickly advanced, sharp nails at the ready began scratching at the metal with loud screeches like fingers down a chalk board.

The second guard shouts up "Sir, a second unit is approaching in from this side, two more of them."

Hobs moved over to see for himself and signalled to Jodie to watch his door. The robots began to break through, slicing with their fingers and hammering at the door with clenched fists. The first door began to buckle as the robots forced an arm through catching the guard with its sharp blade, slicing at his thigh. Hobs ran over to pick him up, then placing his foot on the robots wrist he began to fire on the elbow joint. In a flash of sparks, the limb fell to the floor like a dead weight. The second robot hammers again at the door as it begins to shake loose. Hobs and the guard move back and take aim, the door now scratched and pounded begins to bend under the force of each blow. The one armed robot is the first through the half broken door as the two men open fire on its exposed joints, just like Lockwood had instructed them too. As the ammunition clips emptied; the head of the Doppelganger fell to the floor, then its body slumped lifeless next to it. The second robot made its advance stretching out with its razor sharp fingers, slicing through the chest of Hobs jacket who managed to lean back to dodge the full blow. With a quick reload the two men once again fire at its shoulders causing the arms to drop off, then at its head knocking the Bio-Armour off its face exposing the robots inner workings of wires, pistons and circuits, its two beady black eyes staring at the men as their bullets tore through its skull leaving little behind. The second door now began to give way to the next attack. With Hobs helping the first guard, Jodie ran over to help

54

the other brace the door from the blows.

"NOOoo" shouted Hobs, "don't leave the door unchecked," but it was too late.

The rumble of a large object shook the ground of the lab as it grew closer. With a smash, the door flew from its frame and crashed to the floor, Hobs and the guard dived for cover to avoid being hit as they looked over at the large fist reaching through the doorway, grabbing and swiping in the air for anything or anyone it could grab. With the distraction of the Behemoth, Jodie and the guard lost their concentration allowing the Doppelgangers at the door to break through. The door swung open smacking Jodie in the head and side, throwing her across the floor knocking the revolver from her grip while the guard opened fire on the two robots in futility, completely outnumbered. The first took the shots while the second cut the guard down, first taking his leg then his hand before they finished him off with a blow to his chest.

Jodie looked up as the events unfurled in slow motion, her head throbbing from the blow. Over by the first door she watched as Hobs began to run over to her, while the injured guard gave covering fire. By the other door she turned to watch the arm of the Behemoth still reaching out trying to break it's way through into the lab. Jodie struggled to get up as the muffled sounds of the fight surrounded her she put all her strength into raising her upper body with her good arm propping her up. As she sat up the shard from within her sling fell to the floor, its glow seemed to feed off the energy from the fight around it. From the fire fight the bullets ricocheted off the bodies of the robots toward where Jodie sat. With a flash of light a bullet struck the shard causing a large chunk to break away releasing its energy from the main shard's encasing. The orange glow sparkled like glitter as it wisped around the floor searching for a new vessel to contain it, all it needed was an opening to get in. Like a moth to a flame the energy crept toward its new host as it absorbed itself in through the cat scratches on Jodie's hand. A strange tingling

55

sensation crawled under her skin instantly healing the scratches on her hand as if to lock a door behind it so it could not be extracted out. The glow continued up her arm through her veins, Jodie lifted her hand to watch it creeping up her body and slowly fade away deeper into her skin. Seconds had passed which had seemed like minutes to Jodie as Hobs grabbed her hand and began to yell to her "WE'VE GOT TO MOVE, GET UP NOW."

Jodie came to her senses again as the gunfire and Hobs shouting seemed all too loud. As Hobs pulled her up, she unknowingly reached for the two pieces of the shard with her injured left arm, shoving them into her pocket, then they both ran through the first broken door with the other injured guard following close behind, firing upon the extinguishers causing the pressurised canisters to explode giving them a cloud cover to escape.

Chapter 8
Something New

The ringing from the explosion and gun fire still sounded through Jodie's ears, as the three of them hid within an office in case any of the robots had made it out and followed. The guard was treating his leg over at the side of the room while Hobs kept watch.

The guard, in a loud whisper called over to Hobs "Low on ammo after that fight, I thought you said it would be a scout group. THAT was a full attack to me. Thanks to that I've only got the one clip left."

Hobs checked his supply "One clip, half full loaded and one spare, plus a few rounds for the Rex I gave Jodie."

Hobs looked over at Jodie who looked back sheepishly.

"You lost it didn't you."

"I'm so sorry, I dropped it when the robots broke in, then you grabbed me off the floor before I could find it," Jodie fell silent as she could feel Hobs disappointment.

Hobs began to think about the situation "But we're only in this predicament because they attacked in force not as a scout party, so what caused them to home in on us so quickly? THE SHARD, it must be acting as a beacon to them. Think about it, it was the power surge from that thing that started all this, it might stand to reason if that's what sent them crazy in the first place then they might be able to track or sense it, Jodie do you still have it?"

Without a thought she reached in her pocket and pulled out the shard pieces, dropping the dead smaller lump back in her pocket, the main piece was still glowing in her left hand.

Hobs looked disturbed "What are you doing."

Jodie looked back confused "What do you mean?"

"You with your arm all better or did you just forget about the pain. The shard looks smaller, did any of it break off" came Hobs stern question to her.

"Maybe, I dunno, it could have, yes I suppose but it looks the same to me, why, what does it matter?" Jodie fluttered her words and looked nervous, especially as she was the only one unarmed in the room and she was in the middle.

Hobs raised his weapon at Jodie "I have reason to believe you're infected by the shard, just like the robots, how else could you heal so quickly?"

Jodie raised her hands, the shard glowing in her grip, "If I'm infected then why aren't I under its control like the robots, if it's all bad why am I healed?"

Hobs didn't reply "If there's a chance they can sense it then they can sense you, at the very least you're a liability to this mission now, we might as well paint a big red target on our back and let them know we're coming. I want you to hand over the shard, we don't know if we can trust you anymore."

Jodie began to get upset, ten minutes ago she was fighting for her life against the robots and now the people she thought were her friends were turning against her. She fought the tears back in fear of her life, if she handed the shard over then what would happen to her, but at gun point she had little choice. She lowered her arm and offered Hobs the shard.

"Not me, pass it over to him" as he motioned with the gun barrel to pass it over.

The guard walked over while Hobs covered Jodie, reaching out he took the shard from her hand "Too bad, I was beginning to like you" joked the guard but then paused. A tingling sensation grew in his fingers as he held the shard, its energy began to spread and burn his skin yet he felt no pain, with his gaze fixed he, like years ago with the reporter Mckenzie back at the mansion grounds, burnt to ash silently before crumbling to the ground.

Jodie was even more scared now as Hobs kept his gun pointed at her and gestured to her to pick it back up. Jodie was hesitant, why hadn't it done that to her all the time she was carrying it and if she picked it up now would it happen?

Hobs was losing patience "PICK IT UP" and once more he gestured Jodie toward the shard on the floor in the middle of a pile of ash and clothes. Slowly she knelt down and reached out grabbing the shard and waited. There was no side effect, no burning, it was all as it was before.

"I'm not sure why but you've become a dangerous lady but I'm not going to carry that thing so I guess I need you to transport it for me, so move."

Jodie walked ahead as Hobs followed closely behind, armed and ready. She needed to get away from him. Spying a fire extinguisher next to the stair case doors up ahead she got ready to make her move. Closer and closer she got to her means of escape, just a few more steps and she'd be able to grab it.

"STOP" shouted Hobs.

"Why, what's the matter" she questioned as she tried to shuffle closer to the extinguisher.

Hobs pointed back down the corridor "We're going the wrong way, Doc said to follow the corridors with the least pipes to reach the portal room, we need to go back and take the turnoff there, so move away from the extinguisher and exit doors and don't take me for a fool again."

Jodie lowered her head, her only idea for an escape had been lost when suddenly she heard a young woman's voice, echo around her head "Jodie, run."

Jodie looked around as Hobs watched her, slightly confused "What are you doing, I said we're going back this way."

"You didn't hear that?" she questioned.

The voice came again "Jodie……………run……….NOW," a bright blast

of light erupted in front of Hobs causing him to cover his eyes while Jodie saw nothing other than his reaction. Seizing her chance she turned and ran for the exit, as she approached it opened by itself and the voice came again "Not that way, go in the office to your right."

Jodie changed her direction and dodged quickly though the doorway of the darkened room and hid behind the door, peering through the gap at Hobs who was recovering his vision.

Hobs became furious "Jodie, JODIE! Get BACK HERE NOW!"

The fake sound of foot steps echoed up the stairwell leading Hobs to chase it.

"JODIE, JODIEEEEE don't make me have to hunt you down......
..JO....DIE."

Off he ran in pursuit of the ghostly echoes. Silently she came out of hiding, in case he should double back and find her there.

"Jodie, run from here and hide" came the young woman's voice again. Once more she looked around for a person but there was nothing. With a quick check of her surroundings she slipped off down a different corridor to make her escape.

Hobs
Hobs
Hobs
Hobs
guard
Nº 32
Tall man
Why
can't remember
Him
Why?
I have no memory of his
FACE
Blue eyes
yellow!
Hobs
can't Remember
Hello
there

Chapter 9
Brief encounter

Jodie curled up in the corner of an office she had found unlocked and began to cry. Everyone was dead except for Hobs and even he seemed to have turned against her, so now she was alone and trapped. She sat in almost darkness with just the emergency lighting glowing overhead, the dull thuds of robots could still be heard through the empty corridors, searching for survivors, searching for her. Jodie stared at her hand, the cut now completely healed, her arm no longer painful, she felt strong in herself but she was tired and unable to stop the tears.

As she sat in the dark she heard a strange noise like fizzing. She looked over to where it was coming from. She once again saw a glowing orb appearing through the wall followed by a second, then a third. They glided gently across the room and passed through to the next. Jodie was drawn to follow them but something else grabbed her attention. From outside the room came the tiny pitter patter of something moving, Jodie wiped her tear filled eyes and stared toward the door through the dull light. The noise stopped and the door began to slowly open with the sound of creaking. Jodie braced herself and lowered her breathing so not to make any more noise than she had too. There was no where to hide and the door was the only exit. The door stopped moving and then from the base, less than a foot from the floor there popped a cat's head, a black cat's head, the same cat she had seen before which scratched her. The cat stared directly at Jodie and began to purr as it hurried over to her side and up onto her legs rubbing its head against her. With a loud meow the cat then jumped from Jodie and moved away to the door. Jodie watched the cat as she could swear it was checking that the coast was clear. Turning back it meowed again back at Jodie. Jodie climbed to her feet and went to follow, as the cat ran down the corridor. Peaking out from the room, she saw that the cat was now down at the far end of the corridor about to turn a corner, giving another meow the cat ran off and Jodie followed close behind.

Jodie could feel her heart beating hard and fast and all her senses seemed to be on overdrive, the hairs on her skin were standing on end as she continued to follow the cat, but she didn't know why she was. Her brain did a fast forward of all the events so far if she thought about it for too long she could feel her legs go weak. She must continue, but there were so many endings playing out in her mind, she needed to put them out of her head and stay strong.

Deeper and deeper into the facility she followed the cat, every now and then they would stop as robot patrols walked near, the twisted shadows of their reformed armour stretched across the walls as they stomped past. Through doors and offices, even large air vents, Jodie followed the cat which would turn and meow at her as if to say 'keep up,' until finally, climbing though a large open grill they came to a generator room.

Dropping to the floor Jodie looked around for the cat but it was nowhere to be seen, however someone else was. Over in the corner the figure of a young woman was silhouetted against the wall lighting.

Jodie froze, all she could hear were the generators loud humming which seemed to consume her whole body.

"Hello" …... "hello" repeated Jodie, "you need to leave" or does she, thought Jodie is this another robot taking shape, perhaps she was the one who needed to turn and run.....

There was something that made Jodie approach the figure, there was a sense of ease about the woman and seemed to be of no threat to Jodie, but she could not put a finger on why she felt this way, or why all of a sudden trust seemed to be the only emotion Jodie was feeling.

Jodie walked cautiously into the open area as the generators' loud hum covered any noise and external detection. Jodie waved over to the figure who's eyes, just for a second, seem to shimmer with light like an animal's in the dark.

"Hi there, are you ok?" Asked Jodie nervously, "have you seen a cat come this way?"

The figure stepped forward into the stronger lighting. She had striking green eyes against her pale skin and shoulder length dyed dark red hair with a pair of flying goggles pulled up over her head. A purple tank top leading to a greyish clincher corset, together with fabric braces which had large buttons and a thick black waist belt with a double buckle covering a thigh length tartan red dress, black tights and shiny black ankle high boots. Along with the fingerless black gloves, one wrist length and the other past her elbow, the woman looked like a retro 1940's Steampunk model.

The whole encounter felt unreal as the woman seemed to be more out of place than she herself felt, could this day get any stranger?

"Wow" said Jodie taken back by the young woman's outfit "To quote a popular phrase. Does your mother know you dress like that? It's er….. striking and easy to spot, I'm guessing you don't work here?" Jodie didn't know how else to hide her nervousness, "You do know what's going on out there don't you?"

The young woman smiled back "People don't usually see me dressed in this way, I just like to mix it up now and again, but as for my mother, no, not that I know to, but if you see her then be sure to let her know for me" she joked and gave a twirl "I've lived through most fashion eras and when you put the good bits together, Steampunk says it best, all in one go and Retro never goes out of fashion."

The mystery woman smiled at Jodie and spoke, "Sorry to get straight to business but I need to move things along as there isn't much time, I'm here to help you. I can't really explain what I know but I need you to trust me, can you do that for me?"

Jodie nodded "Yes, ok, the way this day is going, why not. Wait……
..your voice its, familiar, like the one I heard earlier."

Grabbing two large empty barrels the young woman beckoned to Jodie to sit down.

"I need to explain something to you and I need you to keep an open mind about it, ok?"

Confused Jodie nodded and took a seat to listen to what she had to say.

The young woman's face twisted as she thought how best to explain the situation.

"You have a power within you which comes from the orange shard you carry with you. I believe a piece chipped off and the energy released from it needed a new vessel to transfer to. The cut on your hand was its way in and now for lack of a better description, it's magic is within you and you can control it."

Jodie's jaw dropped "First, magic, really? Secondly how do you know about the shard, have you been watching me?"

The woman was a little frustrated about how best to explain and make Jodie understand, "To answer both, YES, MAGIC, REALLY and yes I've been keeping an eye on you until I could get you here without drawing any attention."

Jodie stood up and began to laugh as she walked off around the room in a rant, "This is great, my day just keeps getting weirder and weirder. Everyone I worked with is now dead, the one person left seems to be out to get me and I meet a complete stranger who believes in magic."

"Jodie" called the woman trying to interrupt her rant,.

"….has been stalking me since the start completely unseen."

"Jodie" called the woman again, still trying to get her attention.

"….and the entire place is filled with KILLER ROBOTS."

"JODIE" screamed the woman.

Magic Girl

Saved my life
& Shaved me
Magic

Weird
dress sense

Jodie turned around sharply "WHAT," she yelled but was met with a very different view to when she had walked away.

Back over at the barrels the mystery woman hovered in the air two feet off the ground, her eyes and hair were aglow, and her arms held out to each side, energy pulsing from the palms of her hands.

"Now do you believe me?"

The glow faded and the woman settled back to the floor, Jodie didn't know what to do or say, she was almost scared of her.

"You can float, and, and, and your hair glows," Jodie said gobsmacked. She could feel the weakness in her legs return, it was all to much for her mind to take in. Strangely even though she had just witnessed something she could not explain, she still felt a trust connection and continued to face her new acquaintance.

"Its ok, I'm here to help you and, yes my hair can glow, but I only do it because it looks cool and I had to make you believe me. You have this gift, this power within you too, it's the same energy that healed your arm and hand" said the woman as she slowly approached Jodie and waved her hand gesturing her to sit down on the barrel again.

"Do you trust me enough to do as I asked? What I can show you might just get you out of here alive" she asked Jodie who nervously nodded back.

The young woman looked over at Jodie's necklace "That's very pretty, the silver pumpkin-heart charm your wearing, do you mind if we use that."

Jodie removed it from her neck and held it out for the woman to see, swinging in the air like a hypnotists watch "I made it myself, goes with the matching bracelet, it's a kind of hobby of mine."

The young woman stared at them for just a moment before continuing with her lesson.

"They're very pretty. Ok let's get learning, now place the necklace and charm on your hands with your palms flat and face up together. Now concentrate on the necklace, picture it moving on your hand, imagine the feeling of it as it slides and tumbles from one hand to the other."

Jodie thought hard but nothing happened, she began to tense up but still nothing. The young woman spoke calmly and softly to try and help her relax, "Easy, its more like moving your arm, you don't think about it, you just automatically reach for what you want. It's the same principle here, don't force it, relax and know what you want, not what you want it to do."

Jodie took a few deep breaths and relaxed, trying to picture what she wanted she closed her eyes and breathed slowly. Opening her eyes she looked down and the pumpkin-heart charm was still in the same place. "Not to worry" spoke the woman "have a break and we'll try something else."

With a wave of her finger behind her back the young woman caused the nearby door to slowly open an inch or two, then SLAM suddenly. This startled Jodie, who ducked for cover, her hands ready to block any on coming attack.

"Jodie," spoke the woman "look at your hands."

Jodie opened her eyes fully and looked. As she stared at the back of her hand she noticed a light coming from her palm. Turning her palms toward her she noticed the necklace was now hovering a few inches off her skin. She looked around in amazement as the woman came closer and spoke to her.

"This is your unconscious defensive reaction to danger, or the door slam I just caused, subconsciously you're using the charm to protect yourself."

Jodie, relieved at the news, relaxed causing her hold on the charm to release and fall to the floor.

"Do you remember the feeling you just had?" Asked the woman, "Try to recreate that and pick the necklace back up."

Jodie placed her hand out again but this time her palm began to glow slowly from within the skin, akin to a torch glowing through skin turning the hand red at first and revealing bone and veins. As it grew brighter and brighter the charm danced about where it had fallen pinging against the hard floor as it tapped, turned and jumped around. Jodie pulled her hand away in frustration and the necklace fell lifeless to the floor.

"Not to worry" spoke the young woman, "Lets try to picture it a different way. Your necklace is metal so you need to think of your hand as the magnet, understand?"

Jodie looked a bit exasperated as she tried to come to terms with what was happening "My hand isn't a magnet, it is flesh and bone."

The woman thought for a short while "Magnet, magnet, magnet," she quietly repeated to herself, looking for anything to help her with the problem at hand.

"AH-HA, your bracelet, we can use that. Ok reach out with your arm again but this time concentrate on your bracelet instead of your hand as your already wearing that. The bracelet is your magnet so imagine it picking up the necklace."

Jodie took a few deep breaths and reached out again. The glow of energy appeared once more in her palm and slowly began to move up to her wrist and around the bracelet. As the power grew it began to transfer from her skin to the bracelet, causing it to take on the glowing energy as it wound itself around the metal vines, flower and leaf design until it reached the pumpkin-heart at the centre.

"Now you've charged it up, use it, picture it in your head, it's a magnet and you want your necklace back, so get it."

Jodie reached out with her fingers and once again the necklace charm began to dance on the floor, but this time it moved closer to Jodie. As it reached her feet it flew from the floor into her open hand. Lifting her hand higher she looked on as the charm hovered in her grasp.

"I did it, I DID IT" she yelled with joy as the glow died down from the

My Necklace

gave this
to Ffionn

Pumpkin
Heart

Bracelet

bracelet. Jodie just stared as the charm spun around in her hand like a compass' needle.

"Now, keep that going" said the woman, "come over to this side of the room with me and picture the barrel you sat on as a robot that's about to attack you."

Jodie held out her hand in front of her face as the charm spun frantically around. Concentrating on the barrel, the charm slowed and steadied as a compass would spin to find north, its point now aiming toward the barrel like an arrow head.

"Very good, that's it" encouraged the woman, "Now attack it, pretend you have a gun in your hand and pull the trigger."

Jodie moved slowly so not to get distracted and made a gun shape with her fingers, the charm still hovered is if loaded into a gun barrel next to her hand. Taking aim she flicked her thumb down quickly, as a child would do playing cowboys in a school yard, with a surge of energy there was a burst of light and the necklace fired across the room, through one side of the barrel and exploding out of the other leaving a fist sized hole.

Chapter 10
Last goodbyes

Jodie looked on as the barrel flew over on to its side from the power of the necklace. "Wow" she said as she gave a joking blow at the tip of her finger like a smoking barrel of a gun. She turned to the woman who was smiling back at her. The woman picked up the necklace and walked back over to Jodie.

"Now that you know how it feels it's just a matter of pushing yourself to see what you're capable of. You seem to be able to accept that your magic can give power to objects around you that you can control."

Jodie stared at her hands "Is this how you did it when you were given the gift?"

The woman shook her head "No, mine was through a spell book. It was as if the book gave me the belief to do what I wanted but I had the advantage of being born with my gift, I just needed a way of visualising my power and the book gave me that in the form of magic spells. I came to learn, however, that the words and mixtures didn't matter, it just helped me achieve the results I wanted until I could accept that the power was already mine, just like you will someday. For now if using an object helps to train your mind and accept your power then do it. Look at what you did with the necklace, think what you can do with a bullet?"

From behind her back the woman pulled out Jodie's gun.

"Yours I believe, you dropped it back at the lab," with a swipe of the young woman's hand an emblem of a cat formed upon one side of the handle of the gun and the pattern design of Jodie's pumpkin-heart bracelet on the other.

"It's going to need a bit more oomph if it's going to help," she said and with an infusion of her powers the gun began to change its form.

The revolver changed shape in her hand as the butt of the handle covered over in brass. The hammer morphed into an old flint arm, a gold bracket formed around and under the barrel. On the top was a cog mounted bracket with what looked to be an old brass Victorian telescope for a weapon sight. Around the trigger the metal formed into the shape of a cog along with some of the parts looking more like copper and brass in their colouring and the now flat end of the barrel formed a spiders web design. As a final addition an energy level dial formed to the side of the handle.

Ffion was even impressed, with her creation. She examined the revolver in her hand, admiring the newly-formed weapon before handing back over to Jodie.

"So, want to go for a test drive?" she asked "There's a robot patrol not far from here made up of the ones you call 'Doppelgangers,' I will ride shotgun, just in case you run into problems."

Jodie took the gun back "Ok then" Jodie replied "let's have a test run." The woman led the way out of the generator room with Jodie close behind, gun in hand ready for her first true test. Walking through the corridors, they walked until they found a suitable place to make a stand. "Ok Jodie, you stay here and I'll go and get some targets, just remember what you did with the charm, focus the same feelings into the bullet in that gun." Tying her hair up in a pony tail and pulling her goggles down the young woman skipped and ran off up the corridor in a playful manner to find some prey.

"One more thing" she shouted back, her voice echoing through the empty corridor, "don't forget to take the safety off," then she disappeared around the corner.

74

I call it
The Cauldron

Pumpkin handle
Matches my necklace

the other side
has a cat for
Ifion

Jodie stood alone in the wide empty corridor, revolver in hand. Flicking the safety off as Hobs had shown her earlier, she waited but not for too long. The first heavy footsteps started to ring through the silence. Darting about playfully, the young woman almost danced around the corner as she led the hulking robot towards Jodie. With a skip and a hop she placed herself behind Jodie and grinned "I'd almost forgotten how much I love doing this stuff."

Jodie turned to look at her half crazed grin with a slight concern about the woman's sanity. The dark shadow of the robots could be seen against the corridor wall, as the misshapen figure of a Doppelganger turned the corner, its armour twisted like torn flesh copied from one of its victims when it killed them. As it appeared unarmed, Jodie guessed it had simulated one of the science team due to the white fabric patches scattered over it's arms and body sections.

The woman calmly gave her instructions as a whisper in her ear "Take aim, feel the bullet in the chamber of the gun and picture it filling with energy, then simply pull the trigger."

Bang! The first shot rang out but sailed wide of the target. Bang! The second bullet flew from the gun straight into the robots hip causing a spark and a few chunks of metal to fly off.

"Very good Jodie," whispered the woman softly, you've found your aim, you just need to push a little harder, give that one shot everything you have."

Jodie was beginning to sweat as the robot drew closer, its gaze firmly fixed on her. Bang! A third shot hit the robot's head causing it to stagger but onward it came. Bang! The fourth shot hit it square in the chest, but still not enough to stop it. Jodie paused, took a deep breath and relaxed her shoulders. Taking aim one more time she pictured the bullet and what she wanted it to do. Jodie concentrated as she felt the power release inside her like a flood gate opening. As it increased her eyes charged with energy turned completely white. The gun started to glow, the controlled power passing from her hands as the robot was now closing as she pulled the trigger. BOOM! The shot fired off in a glow of energy with the force like a comet exploding out of a cannon. The shot hit the robot in the shoulder with explosive impact, ripping off it's arm. Jodie's eyes were fixed down the gun barrel as BOOM, another shot rang out tearing the robot's leg clean off it's body, in a hail of sparks like a firework display. The robot fell to the floor and began to pull itself along with it's remaining arm, the fingers extending into razor sharp points as it dug them into the floor to gain a grip. Jodie lowered the gun as it reached within a few feet of where she stood. With one last shot she blew the robot's head off. Jodie kept her stance as she just looked at the wreckage on the floor she had created.

"There you go. I knew you had it in you" congratulated the woman, "Although all that noise is going to attract some attention now" she joked, but in a truthful manner. Jodie stood amazed at what she had done. On one hand, she was happy to have taken the robot down, on the other she was awe struck that magic was real in her understanding of it. The young woman came over to Jodie from inspecting the wreck "Well you sure showed him huh!" she smiled "By the way, I've still got your necklace" and she held out her hand to offer it back.

"No, it's ok I want you to have it" replied Jodie, "you seemed to like it earlier, take it as a thank you from me."

Jodie took the hanging charm and walked around behind the woman to fasten it around her neck. As Jodie corrected the fasten, her fingers touched the woman's skin resulting in what seemed like a static spark between them causing Jodie to shake her hand from the short sharp shock.

"OW, That's twice that's happened today."

In that same sudden moment, the energy from Jodie connected and the woman's eyes flashed white with energy for a few seconds. The young woman pulled quickly away from Jodie and her eyes returned to normal then began to well up with tears.

Jodie was surprised at her reaction and tried to joke about the situation, "What's the matter don't you like the necklace now?"

The young woman now had tears rolling down her face as she broke a smile at Jodie but backed away slightly.

"I saw you" said the woman "I saw who you are when you touched my neck, the connection of our magic merging."

Step by slow hesitant step the woman walked back over to Jodie before quickly throwing her arms around her, holding her tightly, the tears still rolling down her cheeks. Jodie didn't know what to do, dropping the gun she hugged her back causing the young woman to hug tighter. Releasing her arms after what seemed like minutes the mystery woman stepped back, wiping her tears away.

"I'm sorry, please forgive me. I'll only tell you that you will survive this, the rest you'll have to find out for yourself, I have to go now" and she took a few more steps backwards again, gripping the charm of the necklace tight as if it was the most precious thing ever given to her, but still moving further away all the time.

"GO. Go where, I don't even know who you are, why you're here, what do I do now?" asked Jodie in a panic of being alone again.

The woman kept her pace moving further away but always looking at Jodie "You'll do fine from here, I know it. My mother sent me here to help you. It seems funny, last time I saw her she also gave me a necklace. She told me there was a task I had to do, someone special who needed watching over and that I needed to help her when the time was right and here you are. You know all you need to know the rest is just practice" she sobbed.

Jodie felt helpless as the distance between them grew "I don't even know your name, what if I need to call you."

The woman smiled "You don't need me anymore, look in the gun, its empty, always was. It was you who took down the robot not the gun you just needed something to channel your power through that you could understand. I've got to go, goodbye."

Jodie shouted at the woman "WAIT, WHO ARE YOU?"

The woman smiled a teary grin "My name….my name is Ffion, we'll meet again sometime I'm sure of it."

And with that she turned and ran away, with a leap into the air and a flash of energy she changed into a black cat with the necklace charm around her neck. Giving one last look back at Jodie, she ran off into the darkened corridors and vanished.

Jodie stood alone again. Picking up the gun she looked in the bullet chambers to inspect it and as she had been told, it was empty. Looking back up the corridor to where the cat disappeared, Jodie briefly smiled to herself, "Ffion, that's a nice name."

As the low thud of incoming robot footsteps began to get louder and closer, Jodie pushed the empty barrel back and moved further into the facility following the power cables in search of the portal that could drain the shard and possibly bring an end to all of this.

Chapter 11
Unstoppable force meets immovable object

For the last half an hour and several dead robots later, Jodie had walked and searched for a way through the labyrinth of the large corridor networks, following the pipes on the ceiling in search of the portal room, sometimes finding a dead end, others leading to smaller labs and offices. As her frustration grew she was aware that she was still unsure of Hobs location but she was sure he'd be searching out the portal room as well. Her fatigue was also starting to take its toll, she didn't even know what time it was, day or night. In the silence of the facility thoughts started to race; the last thing she remembered was she'd had stayed in bed late that morning till 11am, potter around the house before going into town, then getting ready to meet her friends at the club before starting work. If she'd have known she'd be fighting for her life that night then maybe she could have slept in until 4pm so she didn't feel so tired. Maybe had a bit more to eat at dinner instead of grabbing a sandwich on the run. All she hoped for now was that she could get out of here alive just to see everyone again, but for now it was all about the gun in her hand, the shard in her pocket and the addition of her new magical abilities. Nearby Hobs was in the locker room of a security area. He'd been clearing out any spare ammunition as the previous encounters with the Doppelgangers had nearly cleared him out. It was during his search that he heard the tip tap of shoes coming toward his position. Silently he moved to the door for a better lookout. Closer and closer the footsteps approached, echoing in the emptiness of the silent surroundings until at last he caught his first sight of Jodie walking by. Loading up his gun he quietly made his way to the door in order to follow her. As he watched she seemed to be talking to herself, murmuring trying to decide which way to turn at the next junction. With a loud sigh she walked off around the corner out of view so he made his move to follow her. Hobs took a peep around the corner of the corridor to see if he could catch sight of her again, but that wasn't necessary. With a click of a gun's hammer being pulled back, Hobs felt a change of circumstance in the air as he turned slowly to face Jodie's revolver.

Hobs looked down the barrel of the gun "So, you go missing for a few hours and suddenly you seem to have grown a set of marbles and you even found my revolver."

Looking around he checked the corridors for anyone else, "So, are you alone or have you had a helping hand? Are you going to speak or just stand there deciding what to do?"

Jodie's hands were shaking slightly, it was one thing to aim at a robot, completely another when it's a living, breathing person. She stared intensely at Hobs, not flinching as she hadn't thought any further ahead to plan what she would do once she had him. Hobs seemed relaxed, perhaps trying to throw her off guard, waiting to make his move against her when something else happened she wasn't expecting.

From behind Hobs came a small bright golden yellow floating light. Slowly, drifting like a bubble in the breeze one moment, then whizzing back and forth suddenly as if playing. A second appeared next to it, again bouncing and swaying as if caught in a gentle breeze. Hobs noticed Jodie's gaze had shifted but instead of making an attempt to disarm her, he followed her gaze and expression and turned around to see what was distracting her.

The ghostly orbs got closer and closer as they danced through the darkened corridors, then moved passed them. In the orbs glowing light, Hobs and Jodie noticed a figure in the darkness standing staring at them from the shadows. As their sight adjusted, the artificial eyes of a Doppelganger could be seen as they emitted a glow which was barely visible. It walked forward into the light, like the others its body was twisted and malformed, its fingers were rapidly twitching ready to slice at their soft skin. To Jodie's surprise Hobs shielded Jodie and raised a revolver he'd collected earlier from the locker. Bullet after bullet hit the creature, not one missed its mark. Its face mask and chest were in tatters but still it marched on, raising its hands ready to strike as its fingers cut at the air with a swishing noise coming from the rapidly moving blades. Hobs fumbled as he grabbed some more ammo trying to reload but to his dismay the empty cylinder had jammed shut. The Doppelganger walked on, its bare exposed true face seemed to smile as it neared its next victims.

Hobs was still having trouble as Jodie screamed at him "Use the machine gun?"

"I can't, I hadn't reloaded when I saw you pass, the revolver was all I had ready"

He hit the gun against the wall to try and knock loose the jam. Jodie watched on as the robot's hands rose higher ready to strike, at which point she pushed Hobs, who was off balance, over on to the floor and took aim herself, as the power built in her hands, she pulled the trigger with a deafening Boom! Hobs looked up in shock, the robot had a hole through its chest the size of a tennis ball, as he watched it drop to its knees and toppled face first onto the floor. He looked over toward Jodie still in shock because of what she had just done.

"What kind of bullets are those."

Jodie opened the revolver and showed him the empty chambers "Let's say the shards power has given me a few upgrades to rival these things." As she spoke to Hobs, who was still on the floor they noticed the return of the glowing spectral orbs. They glided smoothly through the air back toward them over the carcass of the fallen robot. As they passed over the robot it's circuits began to fizz with the orange sparks. With what looked like a mini lightning strike discharging out of the robot's body, it grabbed the orbs and pulled them both into its chest. It's broken body began to shake and convulse as its metal limbs twisted and stretched, repairing itself. The two of them backed away as the demonic looking Doppelganger rose to it's feet, its circuit lights glowed from the merged spirits within it and its body had formed horns and spikes, its face more of a skull shape in its appearance, now it's make shift jaw opened with a hiss as it lunged toward them to attack.

This time Hobs retaliated having reloaded, blasting at the robotic creature's neck, trying to break its new armour to expose its weaker connections. Jodie joined in as they were forced to dodge each blow from the robot's hands, slicing in desperation at its two targets. Raising the gun she managed to fire off a few shots blowing holes into its armoured chest and catching it's shoulder, smashing the joint causing its limb to hang useless by it's side. Gaining the upper hand the two encircled the robot, blasting it slowly apart, joint by joint, until it was just a pile of twitching metal on the floor. The glow from its circuitry dimmed as it went offline as the two orbs escaped, whizzing through the air and off down the corridor where another two figures stood in the dark. Each orb was absorbed by the dark figures and their bodies began to twist and shake as their appearance altered. Once more they walked toward the pair, stepping into the light to show their grotesque figures before walking forward ready to attack.

"You got any more ammo, if so I've got an idea" turning to Hobs, Jodie held out her hand.

Unclipping revolver ammunition from his belt he passed it over. Jodie took it in her hands and concentrated. As the glow from her hands faded she passed it back to him.

"Here, try this" she said as she took aim with her own gun to cover Hobs whilst he reloaded. Together they were ready as the two possessed Doppelgangers approached.

Hobs counted down as Jodie's hands began to once again charge up her gun "You ready, on 3, 2, 1 blast em."

In a flurry of energy and bullets the two fired their guns at the robots. Jodie's quick small bursts of power tore holes through them whilst Hobs' bullets, which had gained more power, exploded upon impact with the metallic creatures torso and ripped them to shreds.

"I could have done with some of these earlier. So how exactly are you doing this?" Hobs waited for her answer.

Jodie just shook her head, she knew how she was doing it and what caused it but how could she explain the cat girl "It must have had something to do with carrying the shard for so long, must have done something when it healed me."

As she lied to Hobs a light caught their eye, another one of the golden orbs came in to view, then another and another until a whole swarm seemed to emerge through the corridors, vanishing through walls and the floor as they twisted and spun around made up of all different sizes.

Reaching out her hand, Jodie reached out to touch one of the lights, the glow of light fizzed and crackled as it passed through her palm and out of the back of her hand.

Jodie gave a sharp intake of breath and became teary "Oh my, so cold to touch, like frost. I can feel them, I know what they are."

A rush of emotion swept through her as more of them passed by and brushed her hand.

Hobs came closer curious to what she was feeling "What's wrong" he softly asked her.

The glow of the passing swarm of lights illuminated where they stood as she looked on staring at the beautiful sight.

"Its the people who work here, its their souls, I can sense their feeling of loss……. It's so sad."

As the lights faded away from them a single soul came whizzing around the corner in pursuit of the main group. Passing by them it flew gracefully down the corridor, then one of the doors near to it opened and a metallic hand reached suddenly from the room. With a crackle of

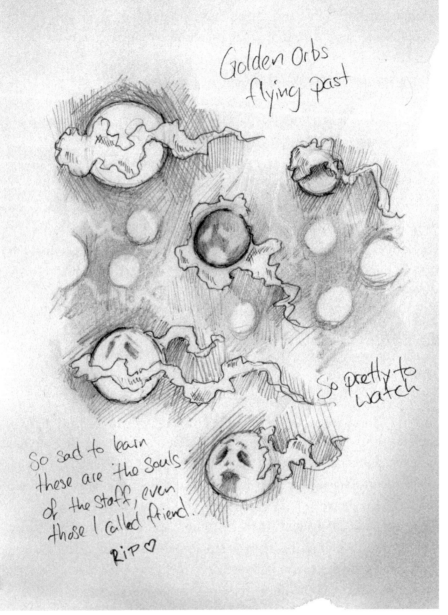

Golden Orbs
flying past

So pretty to
watch

So sad to learn
these are the Souls
of the staff, even
those I called friend.
RIP ♡

orange electricity the small soul was grabbed and slowly drawn into the hand, it's power spread altering the metal and bio-armour around it, making it look more demonic, its body covered in twisted and sharp edges. The possessed Doppelganger walked into the main corridor section and stared at Jodie and Hobs, its eyes aglow with the energy. Assessing the situation the robot began to back away and made its escape down the hallway.

"Phew, it's gone" said Jodie.

"I'm not so sure, there are three things that way" explained Hobs. "First it's heading toward the portal room, second that's where the souls flew to and last, based on the logs I read back in the security lockup, there's a whole room filled with robots. All its got to do it boot them up and its got us outnumbered and with the souls possessing them, we're in trouble."

"Then what are we waiting for? We either catch up and take it down before it can do anything or get to the portal, drain this shards power and hope it shuts everything down." Jodie extended her hands out to Hobs, one open in friendship and the other with the shard in it. "The enemy of my enemy, if you want to help me finish what we came down here to do then shake on it, other wise if you want this shard then we're going to have to fight."

Hobs weighed up the situation and stared at the shard before reaching out and shaking her hand "The shard's yours to sort, I'm in on your little plan."

"Good, give me all your ammo, now we know I can enchant it with power, might as well make the most of it." She set about charging up all the clips and magazines Hobs had collected in one go. The duo then ran off following the pipes to reach the portal room. With the lack of electrical power the lights became dimmer as they got closer to the room.

Hobs pointed out the wall signs, they were not far away now. If they kept on moving they would only have the portal to deal with but they were

87

already too late. Running around the corner of the large hallway they ran straight into a dozen Doppelgangers. All had been recently activated and all in their preset forms, they were not yet equipped with any bio-armour. Standing, looking like reanimated skeletons, they all turned to look at Jodie and Hobs their eyes aglow as they stared at their targets then turned away to look toward a figure standing by a large door at the other end of the corridor. It was the possessed robot, who had used it's head start effectively. Releasing a blood curdling scream, it's distorted chest armour began to expand and crack with light beneath it. Clawing at its chest it ripped the armour open to expose a collection of souls it had trapped. With one final screech the trapped souls flew out and toward the other robots as it dropped to the floor drained of power like a dead weight. The new robots twisted and convulsed as they grabbed the orb souls and absorbed them into their bodies.

Hobs laughed, much to Jodie's surprise "How can you laugh at a time like this?"

Hobs grinned back "The good news is, that's the door we need at the far end."

"And what's funny about that" she ask, charging up the revolver with magic as her eyes glazed over white.

"That's the thing, absolutely nothing" he laughed as he took aim and began to shoot at the oncoming robots. Jodie joined the fight as the explosion of ammunition and magic rocked the walls and floor. The demonic looking robots moved faster without the bio-armour weighing them down. They used their claws to attach themselves to walls and ceiling, jumping around like grasshoppers as they closed the gap on the two survivors. Hobs ran to the side and dragged over a large filing cabinet knocking it over to give some cover. Jodie did the same by using her magic to charge up her bracelet, using it as a magnet to drag loose furniture over as the attack continued with robot arms, hands, legs and heads flew off with each successful shot fired. From behind them came the sound of marching feet. Turning toward the noise they saw a group of eight Doppelgangers approach from behind them, worse still was that some of them, although not carrying a soul, were armed with guns.

"Any idea what to do now?" asked Jodie whilst she fired a shot that blew the head clean off one of the robots as it leapt through the air to attack them.

Hobs was reloading, he seemed to be thinking of a plan when his reply came, "No, not really. Not like it can get any worse though is it?" He chuckled as he began to open fire again.

As the attack continued there came a rumble of noise that shook the floor, the pair looked at each other. Knowing only one thing could make that kind of impact.

"You were saying" said Jodie sarcastically.

The armed Doppelgangers parted as down from the corridor came a large sphere, its body also seemed to be supercharged with souls, it's shell had expanded into segments exposing the electronics inside, all lit up in a rainbow of neon glows. Rolling to the centre of the wide corridor the huge robotic beast transformed into it's three armed Behemoth, ready to strike at them, each fist impacting upon the floor causing it to dent and break up. Running from their cover, Jodie and Hobs split up to avoid the hulking beast's arm as it smashed through their defences with one blow. They both opened fire and sparks flew off its armour plated body.

Jodie and Hobs jumped and dodged the huge arms as they slammed down around them, all the while fighting off additional attacks from the Doppelgangers, in particular the possessed ones which jumped around like fleas, lashing out with their claws, while the others that wore the armour opened fire with their mimicked weapons. Using any available cover, the duo dodged and weaved around the open hallway blasting at everything before moving again to avoid the Behemoth's crushing blows which destroyed what little protection and defence they had. Whilst

Hobs reloaded a sharp pain ran through his leg as a bullet passed through his thigh causing him to yell in the pain. Jodie fended off another attack taking a Doppelganger down with a shot to the waist, splitting its robotic torso in half in a shower of sparks before she ran over to where Hobs was kneeling on the floor, bleeding, as he continued to reload. A hail of gunfire rang out as the armed robots fired at the pair. Holding her hand up in front of them, Jodie attracted the larger metal pieces from the floor like a magnet forming a shield to block the barrage of bullets. Holding the shield she turned to fire upon the other robots to the opposite side of her, as Hobs tied off his gun strap around his leg and reloaded. From behind her came another attack, one of the possessed Doppelgangers had circled around behind and leapt at them. Hobs saw the attack and opened fire destroying the robots shoulder and part of it's face in a blast of super charged bullets, unfortunately the rest of the robot body's momentum hit Jodie square in the back knocking her across the floor, winded by the blow.

Jodie now lay beneath the Behemoth as it closed in on her. One huge arm hammered down on either side to stop her escape as she tried to regain her breath back. Fixing its gaze upon her it slowly lowered itself closer so it was literally face to face. She had no where to go, she stared into the robotic creatures eyes and screamed at it in defiance, her eyes turned white with a rush of power. Lifting her gun she clasped it tightly in her hands filling it with more energy than she had ever charged up before. Taking aim at point blank range she targeted its head and pulled the trigger. The huge beast seemed to express surprise as it tried to lift up and away from the oncoming blast, but it was too late. The explosion rocked the walls as the shockwave blast of air knocked the Doppelgangers and even Hobs to the ground. Jodie slid on her back across the floor for several metres coming to a halt watching the Behemoth rotate like a childs spinning top and then to wobble and tip over on its side, its head and one of its arms completely detached in the

90

blast. Jodie's exhilaration from defeating the large robot quickly turned to dread in a matter of seconds as she turned her head to find she had come to rest at the feet of a Doppelganger, it's claws already extended ready to deal a fatal blow. Quickly lifting her gun again in the hope she could get a lucky shot in, the robot's razor sharp fingers swiped downward before she could even pull the trigger. For that second she blinked, thinking it was the end, only to look up as again bullets began to hit its chest throwing it off balance and knocking it over to the floor. The super charged UMP45 bullets kept coming as Jodie looked over to see Hobs with gun blazing as he came closer putting the last of the ammo in his gun clip into his target. Reaching down he extended his hand out to help her to her feet. Accepting the friendly gesture and for saving her life she grabbed his hand and clambered back up to her feet.

Hobs reloaded, "They're beginning to move again. Quick while we have a chance, the doorway."

The duo ran passed the fallen robots to the open doors finally reaching the portal room, "Find something that shuts the door" shouted Hobs as the machines advanced toward them picking up speed.

"There's no button or anything" screamed Jodie but Hobs had already found a way.

"Grab the crank handle and start turning." He showed her what to do and Jodie found the second handle at the other side of the doorway and helped, turning as quickly as they could to lock out the ever advancing danger.

"Crank handles on the inside, really" she quipped to Hobs.

"Sure, think about it, this thing absorbs energy so the fewer electrical points it has to work from the better."

As the doors closed locking out the angry robot mob they quickly rested to catch their breath whilst listening to the thuds and scratching at the solid metal door. Turning around they stared at the glowing portal hovering in the centre of a very large empty circular room.

Chapter 12
Between a rock and a hard place

Due to the limited low powered emergency lighting the room was mainly aglow with the portals blue light. They were standing on a raised walkway that encircled the entire room with three out reaching walkways leading to the centre and to the portal. Down on the lower ground level were flat sections divided up by pipes and a minimal amount of lab equipment. Overall the room was quite stark and bare.

"What now then, we're here but do I just throw this inside and it's all over?" questioned Jodie.

"Maybe" replied Hobs "Try something."

Jodie made her way along the walkway over to the portal and took the shard out of her pocket and looked at it in the palm of her hand. As if it sensed where it was and what was about to happen, it began to glow brighter than ever, then strange groans from the metal work below echoed around the room.

"Hope that was your stomach Hobs, cause otherwise I don't want to know where that noise came from."

"Just throw it in and get rid before something has a chance to get in here" he yelled over.

Raising her arm to throw the shard, it pulsed as a cable pipe came lose from the wall and swung toward her, knocking the shard from her grasp onto the floor below. Jodie grasped her hand tight from the impact as she looked over the edge to find where it had fallen.

"Jodie, you ok?" asked Hobs as he searched with her.

Jodie angrily mumbled to herself as she found the nearest ladder and climbed down to the floor level below. The glow from the shard gave away it's position in the darkened room. She picked it up off the floor

when suddenly a cable flew out of the wall and wrapped itself around
her wrist and began to tighten, pulling her gun out she blew the cable in
half causing it to drop to the floor.

"HOBS, HOBS,"

"What"

"Did you see that?"

"No, what was it you're shooting at?"

"The wall, the cables in the wall, attacked me, I think it tried to take the
shard when I picked it up" and with that realisation she quickly ran back
to a ladder to Hobs on the upper section, "I think the shard is protecting
itself, first when I went to throw it and then when I went to pick it up."

Hobs thought about the situation "If you'd have asked me yesterday I'd
say you were crazy, but given what we've been through you might have
a point. We might have to put it through the portal by hand so there's no
error."

Jodie looked at Hobs like he'd gone insane "I know it was a while ago
but don't you remember we were told people have gone missing in the
Portal and one man lost his arm?"

"Yes but, they didn't have the shard and only we can stop this from
escaping outside this facility, we're the only one's who have a clue that
getting rid of that ember shard will stop all this in its tracks" argued
Hobs.

Jodie was about to counter his point when suddenly a huge pipe smashed
into the wall between them. It flexed like a tentacle, pulling itself out of
the hole in the wall it had just made.

"JODIE, move around the other side of the room" yelled Hobs as he
picked himself up and made a run for it. Jodie did the same as on both
sides orange energy crackled and sparked as more of the metal tentacles
burst through the ceiling and floor. Shot after shot from each of their
weapons echoed and flashed in the large room as they dodged the attacks
that were beginning to increase in frequency with more tentacles

appearing from the ceiling.

The pair met up on the far side of the room at which point the attacks seemed to stop. Each of them gasped for breath as they watched two long metallic cables unroll from the ceiling and make their way over to the crank handles at the door. Jodie began to open fire trying to stop them from reopening the doors but the room seemed to shift as a wall of metal and wires broke away and twisted, interlocking with each other to block her shots. As the cables turned, the doors slowly opened much to their horror. The remaining Doppelgangers walked into the room with a slow and menacing stomp as they marched inside, their eyes firmly fixed upon Jodie and Hobs location but instead of attacking them they stood guard either side of the door. The cables then reached through into the hall and wrapped themselves around the metallic carcasses from the previous fight and dragged the scrap metal back in and up to the middle of the room to the portal. Jodie and Hobs watched in disbelief as the robot torsos of the fallen Behemoth and destroyed Doppelgangers began to merge and reshape, transforming and swirling around the portal forming a huge twirling ball of scrap. Hobs nudged Jodie to get her attention as he signalled for them to sneak off around the side to the nearest walkway, as they did a large chunk of metal flew at them crashing down blocking their way. Turning around to move back, another chunk of scrap flew at them, trapping the pairs exit. With nowhere to go they nodded to each other, raised their weapons and opened fire. Sparks and chunks of robot parts flew off the large sphere as it still merged and twisted itself into a new form. From around the large mass another chunk of metal flew directly at them. Jodie held up her hands to guard from the blow as her survival instinct took over and her eyes flashed over white with power, the large object hovered in front of them. Inches away from Hobs was a long metal spike that would have pierced through his eye had she not have stopped it. Composing herself her whole being began to glow with power as she shoved the metal bulk

95

back at the portal, the junk smashed straight into it with a booming echo around the room. There came a loud constant scream as the projectile hit its mark, Jodie and Hobs watched in horror as the spinning piles of metal expanded and stretched out then it began to spin slower and slower coming to a halt. Before them now hovered a huge 20 foot head made up of all of the robot parts. Its huge mouth was screaming at them, electrical charges hit the machine like lightning bolts and the portal held within in its mouth continued to slowly spin around. With a turn of its head it brought more of the roof crashing down through two of the suspended walkways and damaging the third.

Clearing the way with magic, Jodie and Hobs began to open fire on the huge head which snarled at them, it sent pipe work tentacles up from the floor to attack, sweeping and stabbing the air whilst Jodie and Hobs did their best to avoid the attack. Over by the door the Doppelgangers began their attack. The possessed robots jumped and scuttled across the walls ready to cut and swipe with their long clawed fingers. The armoured set of robots began to overcharge making their main weapons useless as the bio-armour multiplied at an alarming rate, unable to hold its form but constantly regenerating. The white ooze dripped from the bodies of the robots like they were made of wax melting under a strong heat which caused them to struggle to walk, slowly shuffling along like zombies, their arms out stretched as they moved in for the kill.

Jodie and Hobs took aim at the possessed robots as they jumped and crawled around them, blasting randomly in the hope to get a lucky shot in all the while avoiding the tentacle cables the head controlled. As the zombie robots made their way around the walkway the huge head turned to them and opened its mouth wide as the portal began to fire out soul orbs that had been trapped within the reformed robots bodies within the head. As the orbs hit the melting Doppelgangers armour, there was a crackle of energy. The ooze coated each one and took control of the soul like a parasitic entity. Sensing the souls pain the ooze altered its shape to

96

that of a skull or screaming mouth and other facial distortions as they flew around the room in search of the two survivors.

Hobs was reloading while Jodie provided cover as he watched the souls fly in for the attack like a guided rocket. "That's new, I never expected that could happed," he finished loading and started to open fire with Jodie again. Between the heads cable attacks, Doppelgangers and armoured tormented souls, the pair were beginning to take a beating constantly dodging attack after attack.

Jodie was beginning to become tired, the constant use of magic was draining her strength, "Hobs we need a plan to get this thing in that portal."

"I know. I'm working on it" he shouted back as the blasts from his gun tore through several armoured souls. "Head for that walkway on the other side, you can still jump over to the portal from there."

"Are you crazy, that could kill me!"

Hobs fired off some more rounds, "COULD, exactly, we don't know what's on the other side AT the moment but at least we know there's something, which might be our only means of escape. It's a damn sight more appealing than being trapped here. GO, NOW, this is our chance to save everyone. If we fail now this will spread outside of this facility, until it reaches your friends and family. I'm not going to be quick enough with my leg bound up and bleeding. I'll give you the cover you need to take out the head so you have a chance at getting to the portal, it can't focus on both of us at the same time, once that's done I'll join you."

The head watched on as its attacks continued, sensing that the pair were up to something it snarled and let out a deafening scream. Jodie stared at Hobs, going over the plan in her head she knew it was possibly the only way to do it.

Hobs looked over to Jodie "Are you going to slam dunk that shard down its throat or are we just doing this for nothing. In or out Jodie, because I'm about to run out of ammo and it'd be nice to know whether I might

97

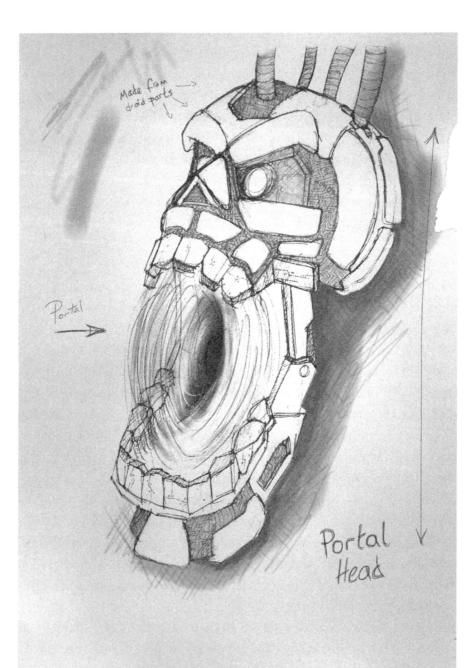

Made from droid parts

Portal →

Portal
Head

die today for a good reason or not" and he dropped the sub machine gun and pulled out a revolver.

"I'm in, cover me" she sighed, then took a few deep breaths and ran for the walkway. Hobs fired off a few rounds to fend of the attackers near Jodie as she ran. Loading his last bullets, he began to fire at the huge head "HEY OVER HERE. YOU WANT ME COME GET ME OR ARE YA JUST GOING TO SEND THESE THINGS AFTER ME TO DO YOUR DIRTY WORK."

The huge head turned and focused its gaze upon Hobs as the robots stopped attacking him and stood either side not moving. As it gave out a mechanical cry several cable pipes raised from the floor and hovered before Hobs. Jodie looked over to see what was going on as Hobs dropped his revolver and the room seemed to fall silent.

Hobs smiled over at her "Told you I was nearly out of ammo."

The first of the cables fired forward pinning him to the wall through his left shoulder as he gave out a scream in agony. A second cable shot forward through his right thigh and now completely secured him against the wall. The Doppelgangers seemed to watch in glee with their twisted faces watching whilst a third cable hovered over to Hobs.

"NOW, DO IT NOW" he shouted to Jodie as the cable fired forward piercing through his chest, with his last breath of air he gasped to Jodie "I'm sorry," then his head dropped forward. Jodie looked on in horror and anger with tears welling up in her eyes, she was now the only person left. The power charged within her as again her eyes turned white and a magic wind blew in like a tornado around her blowing her clothes and glowing hair as she lifted from the ground.

The head turned toward her and scowled as she raised her gun and fired. The first blast went though the robotic eye socket "That was for Hobs," she screamed.

The second blast hit its jaw causing it to dislocate and hang open. "That's for my friends and this next one's from me."

With a surge of power unlike anything she had summoned before, the energy fired from the gun, the recoil knocked her backward several feet and onto the ground again. The final shot had put a hole between the eyes of the huge head. The power seemed to drain from it and it hung limp from the cables attached to the ceiling out of its head. Climbing to her feet she saw the remaining robots begin to make their way around to her, the twisted souls trapped in the white ooze armour began to fly at her to attack. Taking a last look over at Hobs she looked to the portal and ran. Tucking the gun in the back of her trousers she made a leap of faith into the heads huge mouth from the last partially intact walkway. Landing badly on the jaw, she grabbed on to its teeth and pulled her legs up. With one last look back at the carnage she took the ember out of her pocket, closed her eyes and jumped through portal.

Chapter 13
Limbo

Bruised and battered from the fight, Jodie lay on the floor to get her strength back. All around her was nothing, a big black nothing except for the blue light of the portal door she had jumped through to light her way. Still in her hand was the shard which seemed to glow even brighter than before, her vision still blurred from the final blast. She found it hard to focus her gaze upon her hands in the limited light. Staggering to her feet she saw no means of escape other than the portal. Having completed her goal, she placed the ember shard upon the floor and staggered back to the portal light to make good her escape. Step after step became heavier than the previous and the portal seemed to move away from her, even though she had jumped through she seemed to be about 30 feet away from it now.

From beside her she felt the brush of cold air as something seemed to move past her in the dark. Again from behind another brush of air seemed to shove her forward. Nervous from the experience she tried again to make her way to the portal. The sound of growls and hissing seemed to grow steadily as if not one but a group of animals were approaching her. Her pace quickened as her bruised body ached with every impact her feet made. Again the noises came, closer and closer and the panic within her started to swell. Looking ahead to the portal light, which didn't seem to be getting any closer, a flash of claws and teeth raced past in front of her, a tail whipped into the air as the creature crossed her path. Frozen with fear, she stood silently as the noises grew louder and louder. As she waited for something to happen, she noticed a glow coming from by her feet. Looking down she found herself once again standing by the ember shard, its light glowing brightly causing her to catch quick glimpses of what surrounded where she stood but not close enough to be fully seen just on the edge of the embers glow.

"The light" she whispered under her breath and quickly knelt down to pick the shard back up.

"They don't like the light."

As she grasped the shard from the ground the noises stopped, as if a switch had been turned off. Holding her arm out in front of her, Jodie slowly made her way back to the portal only this time, while holding the shard, it seemed to be getting closer. Cautiously she took step after step until she was only a few feet away from the doorway. Like a spinning frozen slab of ice the portal turned around and around, looking through it back into the room was blurry, all she could see was a shape and movement on the other side. As she walked around the portal she could make out the entire room through it, the robots and even part of the head which had all fallen to the floor, lifeless just as they had hoped might happen. As she continued to look around she came to where Hobs body was pinned against the wall. There was something different, his head was raised up and seemed to be looking around. Slowly his figure seemed to grab the cable in his shoulder and pulled it out of his body. Reaching down he freed his leg and last, with both hands gripping the cable though his chest he pulled it out and dropped it to the floor.

The figure then walked to the edge of the platform and with a gentle glide, landed on the other side of the portal and stood outside of it staring through at Jodie. Slowly the figure pushed against the portal, blue sparks flew around where there was any contact, until finally it was through and standing in front of her, silhouetted against the portals light. She shuffled backward in disbelief as she tried to comprehend what or who she was looking at.

"It couldn't be" she questioned herself. "But your dea..," as Jodie held the ember shard higher to light the persons face. Hobs stared back at Jodie with his wry smile across his face, she could even see his skin was

102

untouched through the holes in his clothes where the cables and torn it, but it was all to much for her. Between the confusion and exhaustion of the events that had taken place, her vision blurred as she began to lose consciousness. At the last second there was a look of shock across her face as she thought she caught a glimpse of Hobs eyes turning yellow in the ember shards light.

In the darkness of the portal's limbo, Hobs stood over the unconscious body of Jodie, the ember shard in her hand. Holding out his hand, wisps of energy flew from the shard, causing Hob's eyes to glow brighter yellow as the shard crumbled into fragments in her hand, brittle and void of its power. "Thank you Jodie, I could never have done all this without you" he spoke, his voice now altered in the darkness of limbo.

In the distance he could hear what sounded like the mutterings of a mad man growing closer in the glow of another burning ember, Hobs smiles and speaks to Jodie as if she were still conscious.

"Well, well my dear, its seems we have attracted the attention of my most troublesome occupant and a family friend, but he's not for you to deal with…..yet. I can't let you return to your life Jodie, this is one time everyone must be made silent and, I've made sure they all are except for you. But what to do, I have you right where I need you yet I cannot harm you as you have absorbed a part of my power from the shard."

Hobs paused to gather his options. "Shall I leave you here forever? Hmm, no that would never do now would it, especially after what I've just put you through. Instead I will grant you a life, however long it. might last you, it will be your destiny to prepare the events that have already happened."

Hobs turns to the portal and with a wave of his hand the swirling sparks fizzle and die and with it, all the light. In the complete darkness the air fell silent for just a moment, when suddenly a blue spark crackles into life like a sparkler being lit, this time from the other side of where Jodie lies on the floor. Hobs kneels and lifts Jodie in his arms and steps through the new portal.

"Wake up Jodie" speaks Hobs voice.
Groggy and dazed Jodie opens her eyes to the bright midday sun streaming through the leaves on the branches of the tree shading her. Looking around she finds herself lying against the trunk of a large tree, alone. As her senses come back to her and reality began to settle back in she looked over to her left to a river flowing freely not far from where she is sitting. Following the rivers flow she looks up toward what she believes is a 17th Century English village with its old style buildings, each little chimney pot with smoke coming from the fires within. From behind her she could hear the sound of a water fall. Turning to look she sees an old water mill with its great wooded wheel slowly turning.
"Hello," came a man's voice from behind her. Jodie jumped and scrabbled backwards against the tree in panic expecting the worst.
"Forgive me, I didn't mean to startle you" and he raised his hands as if to try and settle her worries.
"Allow me to introduce myself, my name is John, I walk this way each day to help run the mill over there," pointing to the building behind her. Jodie seemed to calm and stared at John from head to foot. He looked in his late twenties or early thirty's and his clothes were an old style that she had only seen in text books at school or in television programmes and movies.
"Are you all right" asked John softly, "is there anything I can do, are you lost," his voice full of sympathy for the lonely young woman.
Jodie climbed to her feet and looked around once more. "Is this all real" she quizzed, a look of disbelief crossed her face as she turned again to take it all in.
"Yes, yes it's all real" replied the puzzled John, "it's a beautiful spring day, March 27th 1638" smiled John.
Jodie's expression dropped as she felt a wave of dizziness come over her

and she began to stagger. Moving quickly John comes to her aid and steady's her. "Are you ok Miss" he asked politely.

"No, not really" she replied.

John rested her back over by the tree trunk to rest again. "I work over in the Water Mill. I will attend to my staff and then come back for you so we can work out together where you are from. The city perhaps from your clothing" quizzed John.

Jodie smiled, slightly embarrassed by the comment. "Yeah, something like that I think" she smiled back, unable to explain to this man before her what really happened.

John raced over to the mill while Jodie gazed once more over the little village. It seemed to be built within the valley with five main focus points around it. To the left was a hill with what looked like a rock structure upon it like a set of vertical pillars. The next along had a wooden house with a stone chimney poking out just above the tree line. The third main area was ahead of her with a church and graveyard which towered over the small village houses. The fourth had a large building with children playing outside its doors, a school building or hall maybe. Turning her gaze one last time she looked up the hill. Upon it, showing above the tree line, she could hear building work taking place on a large mansion, she seemed to be drawn to it like an invitation to walk over and go inside. From the partially built attic she could see a man in the half built window giving directions to the workforce. He seemed thin and gangly with pale white skin reflecting the bright sun and seemed to now be watching her just as much as she stared back. Not realising, she starts to take a step forward, then another step all the while staring up at the building as it drew her in.

"Glad to see you've found your feet" spoke John with a deep couple of breaths from his run over back from the Mill. "I live in the house up on the hill" he pointed to the wooden house she had only just been staring at. "I have food and water there if you'll except my hospitality, while we find out where your from and most importantly where you might have been going."

As the pair walked off through the village, Jodie moved the gun quickly from the back of her trousers into her pocket to keep the modern technology she channelled her powers through hidden from the locals who would not understand a revolver, never mind why a strange woman to their village would be carrying a gun the likes of which they would not have seen before.

Hobs appeared from behind the Water Mill having watched the meeting from afar pleased with the end result and obtaining his goal.

"Enjoy what you have my dear, for like everything in this world they are always short lived."

As the sunshine beams down, Hobs smiles and turns walking away into the forest. Against the Mill's wall Hobs shadow stands still before it too gives a laughs as it turns, walking away into the forest after him.

As Jodie limps away to the house on the hillside she could hear a chink noise against the gun in her pocket. Reaching into her pocket she pulled out the smaller piece of shard she had all but forgotten about that was tapping against the metal barrel. Curious if she still had her powers she focused upon it, the small piece begins to glow orange then blue at its centre. John looks over to see what he thinks is a gem stone in her hand.

"Hey, what's that, sure is quite pretty, almost looks like it's glowing in the sunlight."

Jodie quickly closed her hand shut "It's nothing, just part of a necklace that broke."

John smiled back, "Well, I'm sure I can get that fixed for you along with everything else."

Necklace
made from
fragment

Main Shard
the cause of
all my problems

Epilogue
Ending at the beginning

8 years later

The night began to creep in as the sun's light set over the hillside. A crisp frosty air glowed yellow, orange and purple welcoming the growing dark sky as the stars began to twinkle. From the house up on the hill, overlooking the village, a warm light shone from the windows and the rhythmic thud of an axe chopping wood ready to warm the family home rang through the silent air.

Sitting inside at the table, Jodie wrote in her diary by the glow of the fire. 'Today I found myself thinking of my past, which is a future that has not yet happened. My life has changed so much, yet I found myself thinking about my old job, Pete the security guard and even Dr Lockwood. All the events that took place and the people that were lost.

It's funny, I can remember the whole thing as if it was yesterday but as hard as I try I can't remember Hobs. I see him only as a blurred six foot tall figure in my memory, no defined face, physical build and even the colour of his hair are all lost to me, but I know him. Each time I try to imagine him the picture in my mind changes as if he had a physical presence like that of a ghost.

I'm sure it may come to me one day when I think again of the future, my past, but until then I know that I am happy here.'

Jodie closed her book and walked over to the front door. Full of love for her second life she looked around with a warm heart, although she was stranded in time, over the years she had come to call this little village home. She gazed over watching her husband collect the logs for the fire.

The man who first greeted her had in time, become her love. Over the bubbling of the cooking pot came the tiny footsteps across the wooden floor, her young daughter came close and hugged against her leg. A moment of peace swept through Jodie as her life was almost perfect, at that one point she felt completely happy.

Looking up, the little girl with big glazed eyes reaches up to her mother "Mummy, please let me wear your pretty necklace" she begged with her large eyes and cute smile. Jodie kneeled down to her daughter's side and took the necklace from around her neck. She held it in her hand and stared into the decorative stone ember that had now been shaped and polished by her husband, who made it into the necklace for her. It shimmered with a brief orange glow as she thought about everything she had been through and the life she had left behind.

The little girl gave her mummy a quick kiss on the cheek "Please mummy can I wear it while I play" followed by a bigger hug.

Jodie smiled and fastened the ember necklace around her daughter's neck. The little girl skipped off to play on the tree swing while Jodie went inside to finish preparing the table for tea. The little wooden house glowed warm with candle light and a roaring fire in the stone built chimney, once again Jodie smiled at her life and how it had changed, that it had taken a complete mishap, adventure, journey or whatever you would call what had happened to bring her to where she was now. With a wave of her hand she used her powers to set the table as the plates and cutlery floated from the shelf and set itself down on the table ready. Then everything was ready and she went to the door to call her family in.

"JOHN, time to eat."

"I'M COMING," he shouted back from behind the wood store.

Jodie looked over to the tree swing and called to her daughter, "FFION, come on now, time to eat, come get warm by the fire." The little girl ran from her swing into the arms of her loving mother as they entered the house.

From down in the village the fiery torches began to light as a crowd gathered. John watched from the house door as he could see the lights assemble and set off to begin making there trail through the trees in their direction. He popped in through the door and went over to Ffion and gave her a kiss on her head as she sat in her chair ready.

"Go in the other room Ffion and play, daddy just needs to talk outside then I'll be back," he smiled softly as Ffion skipped off to get her dolls and play.

"John, is there anything wrong," whispered Jodie concerned as she held his arm.

"Its ok, there is something going on in the village since that Witchfinder arrived, they seem to be heading this way, I'll be outside to check what's going on, nothing to worry about I'm sure," his voice was a tremble and nervous as he turned and went outside to meet the mob. John shut the door behind, unbeknownst to him, for his last time.

Not the End.....

Continued in Book3

Ffion:
Spirit of the Five Stones

ffion ©

Spirit of the
Five Stones Book 3

by Paul Simpson

Prologue
Legend of the 5 stones

October 30th, the original Halloween tale 4 years ago

I was late in the moon lit night as the two teenagers glanced at one another, peering through the bars of the looming gates which stood guard over all threats of the odd abode, yet it opened as the two leaned on it with a deafening screech of rusty metal.

"It's open!" said the boy with surprise.

"Race you to the attic!" shouted the girl, already well on her way.

The abandoned attic was cold and damp from the crisp autumn air. The moonlight shone romantically through the broken roof tiles setting everything aglow.

Their footsteps grew louder as they climbed up to the attic. When they got to the door the girl shouted "Ha! Beat you!" pleased with herself as she turned the doorknob, which was met by a loud creak as the door opened.

The boy fumbled about for his torch as they took pause to catch their breath.

"This place gives me the creeps" he said as he lit the torch, "Let's go back to the others…"

"Hey! I can see the church clock from here" she said, glimpsing out of the gaps in the roof. "Look! It's nearly Halloween! I hope you're not afraid of ghosts!" She teased.

They figured they'd look around whilst they were there. Busy hands tore through all the old junk in dusty boxes. The boy knocked a stack over in his curiosity and on to the floor toppled a dusty old book. He knelt down, picked it up and began to sift through the pages.

"Hey! Come look at this…" he spread the book out so she could look too, as he wiped off the dusty cover to reveal its title 'Local Legends', quickly cleaning off his hands on his trousers.

"It's about our village" she pointed out. They scanned some more, when he became drawn to a page for no apparent reason and to read aloud.

'The book tells of a witch and her daughter. Disobeying a coven's rules by having a child by a mortal man and, as a way of saving themselves, they turned her over to the Witchfinder General who was visiting the village. During the struggle, the girl's father was killed whilst her mother was taken and burned at the stake. The child was never found, but it is said that to protect her daughter, the mother, using powerful magic, transformed her into a cat hoping that she would escape unnoticed and eventually break the spell to avenge her parents wrongful deaths. It is said the cat still visits the standing stones on the hill, where it is believed her mother's soul is trapped until the spirits of the five are joined together… or the Reaper comes and claims his prize.'

Chapter 1
The house Jack built

(1638AD)

The cool summer breeze blew around the hollow beams of wood as slowly the mansion grew from each hammer blow and cutting saw that worked upon it. The little village had never had a building of that size built purely for living in, nor did they complain as it had brought work to them as the owner of the site, although considered eccentric, cruel and very strange, did pay well for the building to be completed to his schedule.

"They say this man, the one who is paying for this to be built is mad, crazy as a fool" whispered the builder to his work friend.

"I've seen him, tall and thin and as pale as the moon as if death has already taken him. I heard that he's built all around the country on different sites and that the devil himself gave him the money to pay for all this after he was tricked" whispered the second builder as they each stared at the other in fear of who they were working for, a cold chill ran down their spines.

From the window above there came a creaky old unsettling voice "Indeed the devil did pay for all of this my dear gentlemen and soon he will come for his payment again, which I fear I will be unable to avoid for much longer. But in building this I plan to make good my escape from out of his grasp" and he gave a chuckle of twisted laughter.

The tall spindle of a man encircles the cowering builders, grinning with a sinister glee with his darkened eyes that further put fear into the souls of the men.

"I am told there are witches rumoured to live nearby, do you know of such a truth?" asked Jack.

The two men began to shake with fear as Jack leered at them with a big twisted grin that only served to make them feel even more uneasy. Summoning up the courage to speak the first builder answered back "Yes, it is believed so sir."

The second man nudged him in the ribs to stop him mid sentence but Jack's attention was already upon his words.

"They meet out in the woods and it is thought that they are looking to add a fifth to their group who just arrived recently, a newcomer to the village, they say they can sense her powers."

Jack grinned "Yes the newcomer, I saw her arrive the other day from the attic window, she was dropped off by an acquaintance of mine, his presence is an unmistakable feeling, how nice he has time to socialize." Jack breathed in deep as he stood up straight and tall, his eyes closed as the sun bathed his face, smiling as the warmth touched his skin as if he was cherishing that short moment, like it would be soon lost to him forever before he bowed his head again back into the buildings shade as he began to laugh.

"Their talents might be of use to me, the blood of a true witch spilled in this area will strengthen the lands power making the link between this and the other side weak enough to break through again. It looks my friends that if I can influence such a destiny then this may well be the place of my return one day" and he gave an evil little chuckle to himself and began to wander away back into the sunlight to carry on his inspection of the other workmen.

"Good day to you sirs" he call's back, not even bothering to turn "but don't you have work to be getting on with, we've got a deadline you know."

4

Printed in Great Britain
by Amazon

75380196R00078